THE A

Edwin Muir was born in 1887 in Orkney, the youngest of six children. There, on the beautiful island of Wyre, he spent his first fourteen years, before the family left farming and went to Glasgow. Within four years, he lost both his father and mother as well as two brothers, and, moving from one grim clerical job to another, he increasingly turned to literature, socialism and writing.

In 1919 Muir married Willa Anderson, and they moved to London where he became assistant to A. R. Orage, editor of the *New Age*, and drama critic for the *Scotsman*. Three years later they left for Europe, spending time in Czechoslovakia, Germany, Italy, France and Austria (where Willa taught at A. S. Neill's school); and it was then, at the age of 35, that Muir began to write poetry. In 1925, his *First Poems* was published by The Hogarth Press. Returning to England for the birth of their son, Gavin, in 1927, the couple began their influential translations from German, including Kafka's *The Castle* (1930) and *The Trial* (1935). Muir worked for the British Council in Edinburgh during the war, and later in Prague and Rome, not returning to his native Scotland until 1950, when he became head of Newbattle Abbey College.

Edwin Muir's literary work includes criticism, such as *The Structure of the Novel* (1928), his autobiography (1954), also published in paperback by Hogarth, three novels and seven volumes of poetry. One of the most distinguished Scottish poets of this century, Muir received the C.B.E. in 1953, as well as honorary doctorates from many universities, including Prague, Edinburgh and Cambridge. After spending one year as Charles Eliot Norton Professor at Harvard University, he settled in Cambridgeshire, where he continued to write poetry until his death in 1959.

THE MARIONETTE

Edwin Muir

Ihr führt ins Leben uns hinein,
Ihr lasst den Armen schuldig werden,
Dann überlasst ihr ihn der Pein:
Denn alle Schuld rächt sich auf Erden.

GOETHE

*New Afterword by
Paul Binding*

THE HOGARTH PRESS
LONDON

Published in 1987 by
The Hogarth Press
Chatto and Windus Ltd
30 Bedford Square, London WC1B 3RP

First published in Great Britain by The Hogarth Press 1927
Hogarth edition offset from original British edition
Copyright © Gavin Muir 1927
Afterword copyright © Paul Binding 1987

All rights reserved. No part of this publication may be reproduced, stored in a retrieval system, or transmitted in any form, or by any means, electronic, mechanical, photocopying, recording or otherwise, without the prior permission of the publisher.

British Library Cataloguing in Publication Data

Muir, Edwin
The marionette.
I. Title
823'.912[F]   PR6025.U6

ISBN 0-7012-0783-3

Printed in Finland by
Werner Söderström Oy

MARTIN SCHEFFER lived with his son in a large square house on the Kapuziner Berg. Sometimes for weeks they did not see each other.

The mother had died in giving birth to Hans, and from the beginning Martin had felt an antipathy to him. As the child grew he saw as little of him as possible, confiding him to the old housekeeper, Emma, and a succession of young nursemaids who never remained long in the house. After it was discovered that Hans was feeble-minded, Martin could not bear to be reminded of him.

Hans never sought the companionship of his father. He avoided everybody. He liked empty rooms, and with the doors and windows shut he sat for hours in his bedroom on the top storey, in silence, gazing at the vacant expanse of floor and walls. The happiest moment in the day was the morning, when he went down the stairs into the empty dining-room. Filled with delight, he walked around, stopping to look out of the windows at the towers of Salzburg, the stream down below, the bridge over which crawled horses dragging lorries behind them, the castle fresh in the morning light on its rock, the green, shadowy Mönchsberg, and the blue, jagged Bavarian Alps. He walked about, whistling out of tune, waving his arms, touching the backs of chairs, and fingering the knobs on the escritoire in the corner, whose cold, brown smoothness sent a thrill up his fingers. When he sat down, the expanse of the long table, on which his breakfast of coffee and rolls was like a tiny island, gave him a sense of space. His father was in the study, Emma was down in the kitchen, Anni, the nursemaid, was sweeping his room.

In the garden, too, he was happy. But if a man or a dog appeared on the hill he went in, climbed up to his room, and, the door shut, waited listening, till, the danger over, he might return to the garden again. Certain things he loved particularly there: an old blackened tree standing in a corner, whose branches he had fingered so often that in places they were worn smooth ; a wall of aged stone encrusted with lumps of green moss; and, most of all, the rusty railings, twisted, hideous, and interlaced with thorns, which ran along the front of the garden. Beside them he would stand, their cruel and harsh branches fascinating him until he had to touch them to satisfy his craving. The touch of inanimate things, of stone, moss, iron, or wood, made him feel secure. It was a test ; he doubted his eyes and had to feel things with his hands to know them.

Flowers delighted him. There was a corner of the garden still tended by a casual gardener, and there, among the flowers, Hans would stand for a long time. At these moments he was happy; his small, shifty eyes became clear and frank ; he smiled, visibly drinking in courage and intelligence. If the nursemaid came for him there he did not run away, but broke into a fit of rage.

But a lizard scuttling across the stones would make the place insecure. He saw nature as a terrifying heraldry. The cat, the lizard, and the wasp were embattled forces armed for war, carrying terror and death on their blazoned stripes, their stings, claws, and tongues. He could only run away from them to the vacancy of his room.

Once when he was with his nursemaid on the crest of the Kapuziner Berg he saw a sight which he remembered always afterwards. The evening was still; the sun was setting behind the mountains; from the town, whose roofs were gilded by the light, came the sound of bells. Beneath him, overhanging a little precipice, lay a sloping bank, very green in the level light, and over it, in silence, three black dogs were coursing. Their snouts tied to the ground, their sides sharpened, their eyes desperate, they flew around in circles; sometimes their paws spurned clods and stones over the cliff, but they never stopped. Round them the turf glowed, every blade of grass glittered with a vivid, wakening green, but they seemed to have no kinship with it; they were as chill and dark as the mould beneath. Hans knew that the ground had once been a grave, and he had a vision of the spirit, a few feet underground, racing the dogs and maliciously leading them on. When the last rays left the mound all three stopped, tumbled over one another, and leapt round their master who was sitting near. But Hans was afraid.

Human beings did not terrify him, but he was on his guard against them. When with kind faces they came up and spoke he looked at them slyly as if to say, " I understand you. I know your thoughts." This look on his face made them feel guilty; their pity, which had been real before, seemed to become a sham. Only one human being loved him, Emma the servant. She spoke to him in a voice which never deviated into warmth, made him little cakes and left them without a word on the table in his bedroom, and treated him as if he were both grown-up and sane. At last she won his confidence.

But he feared the nursemaids, who in a menacing procession came and left. He could not understand their healthy, pleasant faces and their cheerful kindness, so current and sure of itself. He knew it was not for him, but for others.

He read people's faces with a fearful curiosity. He was revolted by their broad, fat cheeks, and their bellies and legs bursting through their clothes. He felt ashamed of his own clumsy limbs, and sometimes he stood before the mirror regarding persistently his broad, red face with the tiny eyes and the insignificant nose, which never changed. Sometimes he felt that this face did not belong to him and was independent of him. Then a desire would overcome him to get rid of it. Gazing earnestly into the mirror he would compress his mouth, drawing the lines tighter, and press his chin upwards with his hand, giving it a look of resolution; but immediately his face relaxed again, vacant, stupid, and hostile.

Other faces he hated for their mutability. He watched the blank flesh becoming animated, and the change gave him a feeling of corruption, as if matter were melting. Propitious or menacing, this change seemed to him like a violence of the flesh; the contortions of mirth were like the contortions of rage. The lines drawn by self-control seemed as dreadful to him as those scored by passion.

But usually he was subtle in his reading of faces, perceiving looks of lust and envy passing over them in an unconscious procession unseen by others. He stood outside, and the faces of ordinary people were exposed to him, just as his was blank to them.

The living creatures which aroused his wonder most were three goldfish in an oblong vessel of glass set into the embrasure of the window at the top of the stairs, a little distance from his bedroom door. He was not afraid of them. Behind the crystal walls, in the dim, glassy-green light which seemed to recede infinitely, as if it were a shaft drawn from somewhere far beneath the foundations of the house, they swam, nuzzling the walls with their tiny pointed mouths, and staring persistently at him with cold, remote, and inquisitive eyes. He fed them daily, and it seemed to him that they knew him better than other people, and that in his own eyes there was a look, like their own, which they understood.

What he feared in the changes of the human face, in animals and insects, was their mobility; for everything that moved was capable of hurting him. What moved could destroy, and all that moved some time did destroy. He had to be on his guard against everything. From the world he turned to trees, flowers, stones, his goldfish, and his room which was like an empty place in the midst of existence; to these and a doll, falling to pieces, the only one he had ever had. With Fritz he felt safe.

CHAPTER II

It was sensitiveness that made Martin Scheffer neglect his son, and a sense of shame. He hated the child at first because of the mother's death. But this feeling was soon forgotten; he was ashamed of it; presently he did not acknowledge that he had ever felt it. He dropped the fact of Hans's existence into an abyss, and in his consciousness the child lay slain and buried. He dropped into the same abyss his memories of his wife. When her image rose in his mind he dismissed it; but this did not bring him peace.

For the first two years of his life Hans reminded him of all he had wished to forget. But when the child turned out to be feeble-minded, Martin's feelings changed. All at once he recognised that his son actually existed, and he was filled with pity and repugnance. He felt now that Hans was his son and his only; the mother had nothing to do with him. He regarded his existence as a thing to be personally ashamed of, and he tried to hide it even from himself.

One thing gave him a peculiar cause for shame. Sometimes when he opened his study door Hans would be in the passage. Then Martin would slip into the room again, or turn the other way and go out hurriedly by the back door, while behind him he felt that Hans was smiling ironically, with a knowledge of his power. Before he reached the bottom of the hill his humiliation would be forgotten; but he would recall it again when he returned. Feeling like a thief, he would slip through the passage to his study, and if he reached it without seeing Hans he would sink into his chair, heave a sigh, and plunge into a work on comparative religions which he had taken up after his wife's death.

One July morning while he sat at his desk the door of the study opened and Emma appeared leading Hans by the hand. Martin looked up in astonishment; no one had ever dared to interrupt him before at his work. Then he noticed that Hans appeared to have a different look. He seemed taller and carried himself with an important air.

Dressed in a new suit of black, a dark red rose in his buttonhole, he carried on one arm a new doll with yellow frizzy hair, a red-coated soldier.

"This is Hans," said Emma abruptly. "It's his birthday. He's fourteen. Herr Scheffer should know."

Letting go the boy's hand she pushed him forward and left the room.

"His birthday!" repeated Martin in surprise. "But, Emma——" he shouted.

The door opened again. Emma's head appeared.

"Herr Scheffer should know!" she repeated, and the door closed.

Father and son gazed at each other. Hans remained standing awkwardly where he was; he did not seem to be afraid. He was like a piece of furniture which Emma had just pushed forward, and Martin, if he wished, could now pull towards him. He seemed to be waiting, on his face an impersonal expectation. Martin was suddenly filled with pity.

"Well, Hans," he said at last, "I wish you many more happy birthdays," and he took the boy's hand awkwardly as he might have taken the hand of an acquaintance. But Hans's hand was heavy like a block of wood; Martin held it for a moment, then dropped it, not knowing what to do next. He had only one wish: to get rid of Hans, to send him out of the room. But looking at him standing stock-still, as if at his disposal, he felt ashamed of his desire.

"Poor boy! Poor boy!" he said. "What can I do for you? What can I give you?"

He rose and began to pace the room. At these words Hans looked at him defiantly, on his guard.

"Who gave you the doll?" Martin asked after a pause. In spite of himself his voice was colder.

"Emma," Hans replied in a muffled voice.

"May I look at it?" Martin held out his hand.

Hans flushed and hesitated. Martin saw that he was afraid he would not get the doll back again.

"Give it back," Hans mumbled, holding it out.

"You needn't give it if you don't want to," said Martin coldly, taking it in his hand. It was a fine doll, with a tunic of red felt, yellow brass buttons, blue serge trousers, and pretty little kid shoes.

"See!" Martin said, beginning to unbutton the red tunic. "You can take this off and put it on again."

"No! No! Don't, please!" cried Hans.

"But I'm not hurting it!"

"Please don't! Please don't!" He held out his hand for the doll.

"There! There! I wouldn't hurt it," said Martin, returning it. But Hans examined it searchingly. He was not reassured.

"Now you want to go away and play," said Martin, suddenly relieved. "What would you like me to give you for your birthday? A horse? A little house? Another doll?"

"A house? Another doll?" repeated Hans doubtfully.

"Or a horse."

"Not a horse."

"A house, then."

"Another doll."

"Good. Then you'll have three dolls. One, two, three."

"Three," repeated Hans.

"Now run away and play. Enjoy yourself! This is your birthday."

With his hand on Hans's shoulder Martin opened the door.

"Remember! This is your birthday," he repeated, as if it were of great importance, while Hans walked away to his room.

Alone, Martin stood looking out of the window. He could not sit down again to his work. Why had he said twice "This is your birthday," and why had it seemed so important that he should impress this upon Hans? Poor boy! what could a birthday mean to him? Could he even understand it? Yet, thought Martin, when I told him to remember that it was his birthday, I felt sure that it would comfort him. What made me think so?

Suddenly he seemed to realise the significance of his words. Could that be what they meant? On the day that Hans was born she had died, and this was the anniversary of her death. It was fourteen years since that day in July, but now his memory rushed back to it as if it were yesterday. He saw himself hurrying through the choking streets in the afternoon heat, the doctor's note clenched in his hand. The sweat poured down his face; his hat cut his forehead as he toiled up the hill in the sun; the gate and the house seemed blank and forbidding, as if turning a new face towards him. He ran up the stairs and into the bedroom, his hat in his hand, feeling that everything, the stairs, the door he had to open, the walls, very bright and hard, were unfamiliar. Margita was half sitting among the pillows, white, and slightly swaying with the pain. He went over to her to take her in his arms, but she feebly pushed him away. All the windows were open, but it was stiflingly hot.

His memory lapsed. When it returned he was being pushed out of the room by the doctor, who was telling him to rest for a little. He went into the drawing-room and lay down on the sofa. The air was stifling here, too. The notion obsessed him that no human creature should be born in heat like this; and thoughts of salamanders ringed with fire, of eggs bursting in African sand, rushed through his mind. He got up abruptly and went into the garden to see if it would not rid him of those deep, internal images.

All these memories raced through Martin's mind now as he stood motionless, gazing out through the window. He felt a little relieved; yet he set his mind to check the stream of memory; he could not bear to recall the later events of that day: the screams, the commonplace bustle round someone who is dying, the moment when he entered the room to see Margita lying rigid and changed. Soon, to his surprise, he found his mind running in the usual channels, planning a new chapter, and he had a slight feeling of disappointment. He turned his thoughts deliberately to Hans again, and now he found that he no longer thought of him as his son and his only. No, he was hers too. The realisation of this for some reason consoled him; he felt more nearly reconciled to his shame and to the existence of Hans.

Later in the day he went out and bought a doll, and on returning gave it to Emma to take up to the bedroom. He did not dare yet to visit Hans himself. In the evening he went up. The room was filled with the last light of sunset. Hans was quietly sitting on the floor before the bed, on which were ranged the three dolls.

"You're very peaceful up here," said Martin.

THE MARIONETTE

He felt suddenly at ease, and sat down on a chair.

"Yes," said Hans, smiling, turning round from his dolls.

"Well, how do you like the doll I gave you?"

Hans held it up in one hand. "It's very nice."

Then with an air of triumph he turned towards his father. "I've three now. Look! One, two, three!"

"And which do you like best?" Martin asked, interested.

Hans knit his brow. "I don't know!"

He pointed to each in succession. "This one! No, this one! No, this one here!"

He looked up in perplexity, then shook his head. "No, I don't know."

They were both silent for a while.

"I'm not disturbing you here, am I?" asked Martin at last.

"No, you're not disturbing me."

They sat for a while without saying anything, like a father and son who perfectly understand each other.

CHAPTER III

Martin's feelings towards Hans changed after the evening when they had sat together in the room. He saw him daily now, always choosing for his visits to the bedroom the hour in the evening in which he had seen him first.

Hans seemed pleased with his father's company, but spoke very little. Both shared the peace which filled the room, but it was like a separate thing, apart from them. As soon as Martin tried to get Hans to speak about himself, he became suspicious, and his face assumed the look which it had when some friend of the family asked him, "Well, have you been a good boy to-day?" Martin soon gave this up and resigned himself to his impersonal communion with his son. Sometimes they would sit in the room for an hour without speaking, and then would part with a friendly good night. Martin felt that so long as he accepted those terms Hans would trust him.

He devised schemes to give Hans pleasure.

There was a small wooden shed in the garden, with a window on one side and a low bench running along the other. He had this swept and cleaned. Then he called at a joiner's shop and gave directions, and in a fortnight a large toy house, painted green and white, was installed on the bench in the shed. On the gables of the house were painted tiny scenes from the story of Hansel and Gretel; the door had a brass knob and a knocker; the windows opened inwards and over them were little green shutters on hinges. The door was high enough to admit the dolls; there were beds in three of the rooms, and over each hung a bell-rope which could be pulled, sending a tiny note ringing, it seemed from underground. The dining-room contained a long, bright yellow table on which were ranged white and green dishes; slender black chairs were set round it. But, most remarkable of all, there were three very small wooden dolls, one on each of the beds. These were intended as playthings for the dolls which Hans already possessed: Martin hoped that they might help him to realise the foolishness of his obsession. It was a faint hint, the only one he could venture to make yet.

The afternoon after the house came Martin went up to Hans's room.

"Come!" he said. "I've something nice to show you."

Hans seemed to be interested. They went downstairs and crossed the garden. Martin laid his hand on the door-handle of the shed.

"There! Look!" he said, flinging the door open.

Hans gazed without entering. He saw the house and seemed to be longing to approach it, but he did not move.

"Come! Go inside!" said Martin. "It's yours."

"It's mine!" exclaimed Hans in astonishment.

"Yes. Come!"

Martin took his hand and drew him in.

"See here! The door opens—like this. The windows, too. These are the three bedrooms, upstairs. This is the dining-room here."

But Hans still hung back, his eyes fixed greedily on the green-and-white house. It was so beautiful that he was a little afraid. At last he cautiously tried the door and the windows, and when they opened, clapped his hands.

"It's mine! Mine!" he cried, dancing about, turning to Martin and pointing towards the house; and he made as if to take it all into his arms.

First he opened the dining-room window and timidly touched the plates and cups; but immediately he turned to the bedrooms, the green shutters, the brass knocker, the chimney-pots, trying to take them all in at once. When the bell sounded, he jumped back. But it fascinated him; he advanced and rang it again.

"What's this?" he cried suddenly. He was pointing at one of the tiny wooden dolls lying on its bed.

"Oh, that's a doll," replied Martin casually—"a doll for the other dolls, you know," and he glanced aside at his son.

"Oh!" said Hans.

Both were silent. Then Hans's eyes embraced once more the complete, incredible presence of the house. He gazed at it, too delighted to move.

"It's wonderful!" he cried.

"And now your dolls can live here."

"They can live here?" asked Hans incredulously.

"Yes. You can put them in these beds when they're sleepy, and they will eat, of course, in the dining-room."

"It's too good!" said Hans, lifting his arms and letting them fall.

"It's all yours," said Martin, walking away.

Hans spent all day now in the shed with the dolls and their house. He could not be enticed away to his meals, and next day Martin had a little table put in the shed, and Emma brought Hans his breakfast and lunch there. But he would not let anyone touch the dolls' house, and on account of it he had his first quarrel with Emma. On entering the first time she had lifted her hands in amazement and regarded the house. But when she went forward to inspect it, Hans cried: "Don't touch it! Don't touch it!" and pushed her away. Emma was offended.

"Master Hans never pushed me before," she muttered, and was sullen for several days. Since the morning when she had taken him in to see Martin she had felt excluded. She had wanted Martin to recognise Hans; his indifference had troubled her. It was wrong, and if it were set right they would all be happy. Now things were worse than ever;

she was jealous of the father, and felt that she was being unjustly treated.

Hans kept the dolls in the shed all day, but he took them back to his bedroom with him every night; he could not sleep without knowing that they were there. The first evening he laid them in their beds in the toy house, kissed them, and said good night; but when he closed the door of the shed and stood outside he felt so lonely that he had to return. The shed seemed very distant from his bedroom on the top floor; at night the dolls' house would be dark, sunk in the night, like a stone; he did not know what might happen there. He could not trust the house yet while he was away from it, so he hastily dressed the dolls again, gathered them in his arms, and felt happy once more as he went up with them to his room.

For the first few days Hans seemed to avoid his father. The house threw an enchantment over him; there was something painful in his concentration upon it. When Martin came into the shed and sat down, he seemed to be annoyed. He replied to his father's questions impatiently, flung the dolls, which had been disposed in attitudes about the house, hastily into a corner, and moved restlessly to and fro. Martin left soon.

He did not return until the fourth evening. But when he reached the door of the shed he hesitated, and instead of entering glanced in through the window. Hans had just arranged the dolls in various positions about the house. One was standing carelessly, his arms folded, against the lintel of the open door. The second, the red-coated soldier, was leaning out of the window on the upper storey. Martin could not see the third at first, but on looking closely beheld him lying in bed in the same room. The dolls were disposed skilfully; they made a pleasant, naïve picture. Hans sat before them, now and then slightly altering their positions.

Next evening Martin went down to the shed again, but as he approached he heard Hans's voice, and instead of entering looked in once more through the window. Hans held the red-coated, frizzy-haired soldier in one hand.

"There! I can make you stand!" he said, setting the doll on its feet on the bench. It swayed for a moment, then stood still, staring with expressionless, glassy eyes.

THE MARIONETTE

"There!" he added, giving it a knock on the head. "I can make you lie down!"

The doll fell stiffly on its back, and Hans gazed down at its wooden face, which seemed to express vexation. Then he took the second and third dolls, set them on their feet, and knocked them down. They lay now on their backs, side by side.

"That is what I can do," said Hans, addressing them. "I am your master."

Martin stole away.

A few days later he visited the shed again. This time he opened the door and walked in.

"How are you here?" he asked, feeling at ease and sitting down.

"Very well!" replied Hans, looking up and smiling. The two dolls were arranged as they had been when Martin saw them the first time; the third was lying in bed. Hans absent-mindedly changed their positions now and then.

"I see Fritz is in bed," began Martin. "Is he ill?"

"No; not ill. He's the oldest, and he must be made comfortable. Karl is his attendant."

Hans pointed to the red-coated soldier leaning out of the window.

"And this one standing by the door. Who is he?"

"He's the master."

"Oh! I see. There's Fritz; and there's Karl. What is the master's name?"

"He hasn't got a name," replied Hans in confusion.

There's some secret here, thought Martin.

"But shouldn't you give him one?" he asked.

"No. I don't want to give him one," replied Hans, turning back abruptly to the dolls.

I wonder if he has named it after himself, thought Martin. Or perhaps after me.

"Well, that makes him more interesting," he said aloud.

There was no reply.

"A mysterious chap!"

But Hans knitted his brows.

"And you're pleased with the house?" asked Martin, changing the subject.

Hans's brow cleared.

"Yes. It's lovely! It's real."

He put a peculiar emphasis on the last word.

THE MARIONETTE

They were silent again, and sat as they had used to sit in the bedroom. Martin chanced to remember the tiny dolls he had given Hans. He looked round, but could not see them. At last he perceived them lying on the bench in the corner of the shed. He did not dare to ask about them.

The next time he visited Hans they had gone. Only weeks afterwards did he find them pushed away under a stone in a corner of the garden.

He did not think of burying them, he thought, but they must have troubled him.

CHAPTER IV

SINCE the time when Hans had turned out to be feeble-minded he had never been in Salzburg. His nursemaids had taken him for evening walks to the top of the Kapuziner Berg, not far from the house, where few people were to be met. After (when he was ten) the last of the nursemaids had left, he had never gone beyond the gate. He remembered being taken long ago through the streets to a place full of statues, fountains, and green turf, and being held up to look over a parapet down into pale green water which continually changed and escaped from his eyes. This was the river Salzach, which he could see every day from his bedroom window, but he could never believe that it was the same.

Martin resolved to get him to go for a walk. His seclusion in the bedroom and the shed closed him in upon himself. He would never improve unless he were taken out.

When Martin suggested that they should

go to the top of the Kapuziner Berg, Hans eagerly agreed. But as soon as he was past the gate and found himself on the vacant hill he became excited. He began to make ducking motions with his head, like those of a rabbit scurrying into its burrow, and shrank into himself as if he were trying to become invisible. Martin had to turn back. For several days Hans went about in sullen silence; he felt he had been personally humiliated. He looked more stupid.

But Martin did not give in, and Hans was willing to try again. The second attempt was once more unsuccessful, but the third turned out to be easy. At the start Hans began to recognise rocks and turns in the path which he had seen before. At first he regarded these suspiciously, but presently began to approach them with confidence, pausing now and then to point them out proudly to his father. When they reached the top of the hill he gave a cry. Salzburg lay changed beneath them; the little distance they had ascended made everything smaller. The castle was as tiny as a chessman; the Dom and St. Peter's were delicate and snow-white, like toys just set down among the houses; the tossing shapes of the Baroque Kollegien Kirche, so frightening from his window, seemed quaint and harmless here.

"Look!" he cried. "I can cover them all with my hand." He held his hand up before his eyes, as he had once seen one of his nursemaids doing.

The short ascent had removed the nearness and the menace. The whole town was changed. He realised that it was not so frightening as it had seemed; it had deceived him. He turned to Martin and laughed.

Now they walked to the top of the hill every evening. Hans was much better. He paid less attention to his dolls, and spent hours in the garden, hovering by the gate and often looking up the hill. When his father came for him every evening he was ready, impatient to get to the top at once.

One evening while they were sitting there Martin pointed to a higher hill a little distance away.

"Do you see that?" he asked. "That's the Gaisberg. Would you like to go there? You can see far farther than you can from here. Salzburg is so small that you can cover it with your little finger."

"Can people go up there?" asked Hans in astonishment.

"Of course they can."

"Could we go now?"

"No, we couldn't go now. It takes a whole day to go there and come back again. We would have to start in the morning."

"But why? It's not far from here. Look!" Hans pointed excitedly with his finger. "It's not far. Only a few minutes. We could go now."

"It's far farther away than you think. You can't walk straight up the side of it. There, do you see that path running along there? It's like a white line. Well, you have to go along there a good distance, and then you have to turn the other way, and for the last part you have to climb. But before you can even get to that road you have to walk quite a long distance through the valley down there. And first of all you have to go through a part of Salzburg."

"We have to go through Salzburg?" asked Hans in surprise. The difficulty of reaching the mountain made it more wonderful, and seemed part of its mystery. But that they had to go through Salzburg, which lay in the opposite direction, was strange.

"We have to go through Salzburg?" he asked again.

"Only a little part of it. Ten minutes will take us out of the town. Then we'll be in the country all the time."

Hans continued to gaze at the mountain.

"Well! Shall we go?" asked Martin. "I'll take you to-morrow, if you like."

"Oh, yes! Let us go!"

It was a cool morning in late September when they started; the murmur of the town became louder around them as they passed the cloister and went down the stony, winding stairs past the twelve stations of the Cross. At the pictures on the wood Hans looked watchfully, his eyes never leaving one until it was left behind and another approached. The brutal-limbed Roman soldiers, Christ with His half-naked body sprinkled with blood, the blue robe, the Cross clean and planed as if just out of a joiner's shop: these seemed to have a different life from the walls and trees around them; they were like living things hacked off into jagged squares and blossoming now with a second life, the scarlet blood gleaming upon them in terrible brightness. Hans lingered when he came to the last one, but Martin urged him on.

They passed under an arch of rock cut out of the hill; the stairs descended steeply, and they burst out of the gloom into the clatter of Elser Gasse. The sun beat down on the pavements, the shop-windows filled with glittering wares, the names and names and names above shop-doors, the roofs tossing away. Two gigantic horses, glittering in their harness, swept past, drawing a heavy lorry which seemed to grind and flatten the cobbles. Hans looked up at the houses towering above him; they seemed to be toppling at every moment; they would fall on him. Everywhere were people; dogs ran about; laughter came out of the dark, yawning door of a café across the street. Grown men and women passed by without looking at him, as if he were not there, or they looked for a moment and paid no attention. Martin was afraid that he would turn back.

"This is the worst part," he said. "If

you walk fast for two minutes we'll be in a quiet street. Keep close to me. See, the people are paying no attention to us."

He took Hans's arm. Hans let himself be led through the noise which deafened his ears and the throng on the pavement which seemed to be bearing down on him, but at the last moment passed harmlessly by. He could not distinguish clearly the separate figures; everybody seemed to have a white face and to be dressed in black. A carter on a lorry, in his trousers and shirt, his hairy arms bare, and with a heavy moustache on a grimy face, seemed like an evil figure come out of his dreams. The castle from down here looked monstrously high, as if hanging from a ledge of air; the confusion of roofs and towers on the other side of the river seemed mad and unstable, as if continuously tossing upwards. The shop-windows passed him in a dazzling line, a thousand objects in them, not one of which he could catch with his feverish mind. But he was most confused by the people on the pavements, walking or standing, all in black with white faces, almost all silent. He had to pass through them.

Suddenly he was walking beside the river,

a railing on his right hand, a row of tall, silent houses on his left. The noise fell away behind him; in front there was silence; the crowds had disappeared. Only far away he saw the small figure of a man coming towards him on the immense, vacant strip of pavement, and this man, because he was alone, had a strange importance. Hans watched him approach with a more oppressive fear than he had felt among the crowds. The man seemed to take an endless time to reach them; but he moved aside as he neared and made way, not even looking. To Hans this seemed strange but pleasing, like something in a dream. He grew confident; the next man who appeared on this pavement would make way and pass him in the same manner. He stopped at last, leant over the railing, and looked down into the pale green river careering past him. It was the same. Continually changing, the current formed here and there little knobs which spun round and vanished immediately. The river seemed to flow onward and return upon itself at the same time, with an unwearying, steady haste.

Soon the houses stopped and they were walking through a valley between bulging green hedges. On the banks running along the road, among tall grasses, yellow and purple flowers were standing, gritty with dust, and motionless. Dust powdered the underside of the hedge and lay, soft, thick, and still, as if each particle were very heavy, on the road. To the left the red roofs and chimneys of a row of houses advanced towards them above the hedge-top, then receded and disappeared among the interwoven leaves. They turned into a dark, thick grove of pines, and went out of the sunlight. Piles of brushwood lay on the black, peaty soil; colonies of tiny toadstools stood here and there in circles; their footsteps became loud. Hans drew closer to his father.

"We'll soon be out of this," said Martin.

As he spoke a pine-cone fell from a high branch with a clatter, sending echoes flying through the trees. They were already on the ragged border of the wood, and Hans looked back. That had been intended for him, but it had come too late, and he had escaped. Yet it was a warning. He must take care.

Presently they struck a bare, rocky path and came upon a house. It had no outer enclosure, and the mountain grass lapped against its walls and seemed to run through the door, which was closed. Hans seemed to see the grass inside the house, carpeting the rooms, running up the stairs, stifling everything, and, looking at the bare outer walls and knowing this, he was afraid. The trees were gone; above and beneath them were slopes of grass, not cut into fields, but sweeping evenly on as if with invincible power. He looked around, searching for a clump of trees or a wall, behind which he might take refuge if he need.

"Look!" said Martin. "We're a long way above Salzburg already."

The whole landscape had receded.

"Yes, it's nice," Hans replied, looking fearfully around him.

Soon they turned to the left and entered an open grove of pines. Though nothing could be seen from here, the air was keener, and Hans had a sense of height. But the grove ended in the gate of a field, black and miry, and trampled by the cloven hooves of cows. The marks were innumerable but distinct, and the mire was pitted by little black cups filled with water. The hoof-prints seemed to be menacing Hans: they were like a written warning, left there for him, which he could not decipher.

"Come, it's only mud," said Martin. "We really must pass through here. It's the easiest way."

Knitting his brows, Hans carefully advanced one foot. But the mire seemed to be dragging him down; his foot became heavy.

"I can't! I can't!" he cried, and he began to wipe his boots on the grass, frantically trying to rub off the mud.

"But you want to get to the top?"

"Yes, I want to. But I can't go past that!"

"Well, we'll have to go round," said Martin.

At the end of the field Martin found a grassy path leading up the hill. The trees were now left behind, and the broad brow of the mountain rose before them. Hans was silent, but continued to ascend, looking round as if measurelessly surprised. When they reached the first stage of the ascent, to their right a new range of mountains was seen. Far away, beyond the nearer hills, these gleamed reddish and pale, with a dry, sandy, unnatural look. Seen from this height, their sides and shoulders were bared, and they seemed to be rushing down with a perpetual, dizzy motion into chasms which could not be perceived.

"They're mountains too!" said Hans in amazement. To him it was as if something naked and secretive in the earth had risen and shown itself. But it was not meant to be seen.

Their ascent soon hid these mountains again. Suddenly they were on the crest. They walked across a little plateau of springy turf; the landscape rose continuously before them, gradually tilting up, smoky in the distance, clear and with innumerable glittering points nearer at hand. At last they stood on the edge of the plateau looking down at Salzburg and the plain. Martin glanced aside at Hans. He seemed to be discomfited. Salzburg was smaller than could have been conceived; it was unreal, a trick had been played on him. From here the castle and the Dom were scarcely visible; the tiny fields, cut into squares by the height, were smooth, hard, and planed, like a green board. The mountains farther away had sunk and flattened, as if sloping backwards impotently over the horizon. Only the pine-forests hanging from the sides of the hills were real; very small and feathery, they remained unchanged. In the immensity of the landscape everything was small, hard, and without meaning.

"Don't you like it?" asked Martin.

"No!" Hans walked away from the edge and his father followed him.

Hans stopped. "Can we go back now?" he asked.

"Of course, my dear boy! Whenever you like. Come, let us go!"

The crest of the hill was quite bare, and its uneven shapes seemed to swell and rise at Hans. His footsteps rang loud on the rocky path, as if in this emptiness the smallest secret sound could not be concealed. Above the bare summit the sky was blank and bright; and the hill-top seemed now to be very high above the plain.

All at once Hans began to hurry downward, half running, trying to put the mountain behind him and to regain the garden and the house at once. Half-way down he stumbled over a rock and fell, and scrambling to his feet, he was brought up: he knew that he could not reach his home for a long time yet, and he began to be frightened. Martin took his arm and continued to hurry him down the hill.

"Won't you stop and have something to eat?" he asked.

"No, no! Not here!" Hans looked around and tugged at his father's arm.

Stumbling, they soon reached the end of the rocky track and were going along the grassy path between the fields. Hans walked more slowly. The mountain behind him, he felt that everything had become real again, as it had been before. He need not hurry so fast. But soon he reached the entry to the field trampled black by the cows, and all the things he would have to pass before he reached his home came into his mind: the empty house among the grass, the blackened grove which spoke when you had passed through it, the dogs and black-coated people in the streets. He hurried past the gate and found himself, as in a haven, in the tall pine-wood.

The wood was very still; a faint wind came and went, rustling the brown pine-needles, lifting them softly and letting them fall; as if motionlessly alighted, the sunshine slept on the gleaming brown trunks. If I could only stay here and not go farther! thought Hans. He felt he could not face the remainder of the road, knowing what he had to pass.

Turning aside from the path into the shadow of two pines, they lay down, and Martin took out sausages, bread, and beer. Hans ate and drank apathetically, his back against a tree. After he had finished, he turned to his father.

"Can we stay here for a little while?"

"Of course! An hour. Two hours, if you like. You'll feel better about it in a little. There's nothing at all to be afraid of."

They remained in the wood resting for a long time. Hans became calm again. He lay on his back gazing at the sky which showed here and there through the high branches; he seemed to have forgotten everything. At last Martin arose.

"We'll really have to go."

He looked down at Hans.

"It won't take long. We can go down in half the time we took to come up."

Hans got up unwillingly. When they reached the border of the wood he lingered, and as they issued into the open it was as if they were plunging into a void.

While they had been in the wood, clouds had gathered, and now filled the sky. The landscape was overcast; before them the castle of Salzburg looked inky black and very near against the smoky black of the mountains, which seemed to be just behind and almost touching it; one shaft of light quivered on a hillside over the valley. Rain began to fall; it increased and came down in torrents. The roads were presently soft and slippery. Hans walked on in dejection, noticing nothing. A man with a gun on his shoulder passed them going up the hill, a black dog at his heels. The dog leapt out at Martin, wagging its tail, but as soon as it saw Hans began to bark persistently. It kept on barking until the man ordered it to heel. Meantime Hans had gone quickly ahead, casting glances over his shoulder, and Martin found him standing farther on, trembling, in the middle of the path. He looked at his father accusingly, but did not say anything.

A little farther down he halted and stood still. He was looking at a little squat reptile, its head and neck pointed, its back spotted with yellow and black, which was hurrying past his feet into the ditch, paying no attention to his presence. It was a salamander, brought out by the heavy rain.

The luck is dead against us, thought Martin.

"That little creature can't hurt you," he cried. "It's quite harmless."

But Hans seemed rooted to the spot, his eyes never leaving the little creature at his feet. In the dim thundery light the salamander seemed very bright and malignant, its back scrawled with twisted signs. All at once Hans began to walk on rapidly. But now there were salamanders everywhere; they scuttled and splashed across the road and slid into the ditches, intent on their errands, as if Hans and Martin were not there. At a point in the descent they ceased to appear.

Hans was now soaked to the skin and exhausted. He had scarcely said a word since they had left the pine-wood; he seemed concentrated on the effort to go on until he should reach his room again, where he would be safe. At a village which they were approaching Martin resolved to hire a conveyance. He left Hans in the fireless parlour of the inn, after forcing him to swallow a glass of brandy. He returned in a few minutes with a taxi, and bundled Hans into it. They were driven through rows of pine-trees, black in the rain, and showering rills of water from their branches. The streets of Salzburg began to slide past; they were deserted; a few lights glittered behind the streaming panes of the shop-windows. Martin led Hans up the stairs, past the stations of the Cross, over the hill, through the gate, and into the house. He handed him over to Emma.

"He must have a hot bath," he said. "And then put him to bed."

He felt exhausted, as if by a prolonged mental labour against time.

CHAPTER V

NEXT morning Hans did not get up. He was feverish; the doctor announced that he had congestion of the lungs. Emma and Martin took watches by his bed. Awake he was docile, but his sleep was disturbed by dreams. Sometimes he started back into a corner of the bed, and pointing with his finger, stuttered something that sounded like "It! It!"

In two weeks the first danger was past, and in a month he was out. He had grown during his illness, and was now as tall as his father. His mind seemed to have become feebler. His movements were dislocated, his eyes vacant. He had always talked in a peculiar way; he never gave the natural response to an enquiry, but set himself to reply to its formal content. Now he had to struggle to comprehend every question, and his replies were sometimes irrelevant.

His illness had first made him very thin,

but by the time he left his bed he was plump and white. His sudden growth accentuated the feebleness of his mind. His body, grown to adult size, seemed less animated by intelligence. He has grown to be a man, Martin realised suddenly, and he has remained a half-wit; and immediately afterwards he thought: I am responsible for him now as long as he lives. Hans could look his father straight in the eyes now, instead of gazing up at him from below, and this embarrassed him. Martin caught him several times regarding him with a surreptitious, questioning look.

Hans did not mention his journey to the Gaisberg, nor ask to be taken again for his evening walk. His mind seemed to have returned to the period before the walks began. Towards his father he was friendly, but it was as if their companionship were just beginning. His dolls had been brought up to his room during his illness, but he had not asked for the dolls' house. When he entered the shed for the first time after getting up he seemed to be surprised to see the house there. After a moment of hesitation he recognised it, but without much pleasure.

He had fits now in which he maltreated his dolls. He felt that they should have saved him from his hours of terror on the Gaisberg, and he tried to make them suffer as he had done. Fritz lost an eye, and Karl a leg and an arm. After beating them, Hans was contrite, but his rages returned.

He seemed to be confused by the sudden growth of his limbs. They made him feel more helpless, but he knew indistinctly that they gave him more power, too.

As the winter wore on he gradually improved. Father and son went up the Kapuziner Berg again. Hans looked now without interest at the castle and the roofs of Salzburg, but he liked the walk, and knew every tree and rock along the path. It was too cold for him to sit in the shed. Accordingly the dolls and the dolls' house were installed in his bedroom, but although he spent all his time there he paid little attention to them. Sometimes he sat mute and vacant; sometimes he walked restlessly to and fro as if seeking release.

Martin told him fairy-stories to interest him. But he would not listen; he seemed to think that his father was deceiving him, and stared at him suspiciously. It was only when Martin related the story of Gulliver among the Lilliputians that he became attentive. After this he returned to his dolls. He half-believed, half-pretended that they were real. But they did not satisfy him, and sometimes he hoped that behind a bush in the garden or on the path to the top of the hill he would find a real Lilliputian, who could speak, run, eat, drink, obey, and love him. He would be kind to it, but it would have to be obedient.

For some time Martin had been trying to persuade him to go to the marionette theatre in Salzburg. He thought he could obtain a private performance. For Hans with his love for dolls it would be a wonderful experience; it might even change the course of his life. Martin became obsessed with the desire to show him the marionettes. Sometimes he feared its effect on him, sometimes he set great hopes on it; but what moved him most of all was a curiosity, which he did not admit to himself, to know what Hans would do when he saw the marionettes. But Hans thought of Salzburg with terror. The horses with hooves like blocks of polished stone, the silent people in black clothes, the roofs zigzagging in the sky, the rows of gaping windows, the narrow doors from which people issued out of blackness into light, suddenly appearing stock-still and staring on the pavement—these were far away and he would never venture among them again. But after he heard of the Lilliputians his desire to see the marionettes grew.

Spring was advancing. Soon, Martin told him, the marionette theatre would be closed for the summer, and the marionettes laid away in a dark room.

"Can we go quickly past?" asked Hans. "Will it take long?"

"We'll walk fast. And it's hardly any distance. Far less than the first time. Why, it's not so far as from here to the river."

"We could go past without seeing anything if we tried?"

"Close your eyes if you like. I'll lead you. And then, think, you'll see the marionettes."

"I'll see them by myself? There will be nobody else there?"

"Nobody but me."

Hans thought for a moment.

"I must go! Let us go to-day!"

THE MARIONETTE

"But I don't know whether Herr Hoffmann will be able to show us them to-day! I'll have to see him first."

"It must be to-day. I don't know about to-morrow."

"H'm!" said Martin. "If Herr Hoffmann can do it, will you be ready to go whenever I ask you?"

"Yes, I'll be ready."

"Well, I'll see what can be done," said Martin.

In an hour he walked into the shed where Hans was moving about restlessly, his hands in his pockets.

"Come!" he said. "Are you ready? We're to go at once."

Hans hastily put on his cap and buttoned his jacket. He was pale.

The clocks struck three as they walked down the hill. It was a warm, clear spring afternoon. As they descended, the spires and roofs mounted towards them, their colours softened; the street sounds came up muffled and subdued. The stations of the Cross seemed melancholy and ruinous in the soft air, the wood crumbling and rotten, the figures very old, as if weary of their stations. The Roman soldiers and Christ under His burden seemed to suffer equally, hanging outwards from the heavy, motionless squares of wood. They looked as if they had been trying to say something, but long ago they had given up their wish, and now they were mute and resigned for ever. They passed one by one, gazing through Hans with mournful, fixed eyes, and when the last one receded he felt he had left the final image of safety behind.

The ordeal he had to face arose immediately before him now, as he stumbled down the last steps through the tunnel of rock to the street. The noises became separate. They rose now together, now one after another; he heard the barking of dogs, the crunching of wheels, the clang of iron, the continuous indistinct shuffling of feet, a woman calling to her child, a man laughing. All these sounds seemed urgent; he could not walk forward and ignore them. He had to pass through those streets again. He had done so once and been terrified; now he had to do it a second time, knowing that he would be terrified. Rage arose in him along with the terror which the first separate sounds set vibrating.

They emerged into Elser Gasse. It was

unexpectedly quiet; very few people were about. Hans could see them distinctly, some standing at shop-windows, others walking slowly, those far away on the pavement very small and black. The vacancy of the street made the unbroken rows of buildings more menacing. They thrust buttresses out into the pavement; they intercepted and turned aside the tiny figures walking down below. A little distance away the street twisted to the right, and the powerful, circular slew of the walls gave them a pitiless look.

"Are you ready?" asked Martin. "Let us make a dash for it!"

They walked rapidly across Elser Gasse and turned up a narrow lane with blackened, irregular buildings advancing into the pavement and falling back into little treacherous bays. From a door ran a flight of steps. Hans had to avoid it, going into the road; it looked arrogant and malicious. His eyes fixed on the pavement, he saw the bases of the buildings sliding past, lines of ancient, sooty brick alternating with white, polished block stone; dust and scraps of paper moved softly and restlessly in the corners. Suddenly he felt they were in an open space, and looked up.

On the left lay a square with green trees and seats, and beyond it he saw the castle, the old town bursting with towers, and the blue crests of the distant mountains. Forgetting where he was, he paused for a moment; this spectacle, breaking upon him, seemed like a revelation of the world. But the sounds of the street, which had become faint, gathered again and beat against him; he started forward, his eyes once more fixed on the pavement. Now he saw legs and feet moving in all directions, going out from him in an irregular, wavering circle; the small, rounded cobbles rose and fell; the pavement slid past, running away steadily; then the light became dark. They had turned into an entry.

"We are there," said Martin. "It wasn't far, was it?"

They walked over cobble, and came into the light again. On the left was an open door, gaping into blackness. Out of it came a man with black hair, black beard, and black eyes, dressed in a brown tweed suit.

"You have come!" he said with a smile which embraced both of them.

"It's very kind of you, Heinrich," said Martin.

"Oh, I always like to set them going. Come inside."

They entered a tunnel of darkness which immediately opened into a lofty room a little less dark. Rows of chairs, vacant and regular, stretched away, faintly gleaming, into gloom which could not be pierced. The arched roof was faintly discernible, an overhanging oval. A dry, musty smell permeated the gloom, new to Hans, but pleasant, like an old spice which, losing its scent, had crumbled to dust. The gloom was not like the void darkness of night, but like a tranquil cave of motionless air.

"I'll take you to your seats," said Hoffmann. His voice was subdued. "You see best in the third row, a little to the side. These are the two best seats in the house. I've tried them myself."

They sat down.

"Now, if you'll wait a minute, I'll begin. The pianist has come, so everything will be complete. We'll give you a good show. I've arranged to put on 'Faust.' That will do, won't it?"

"Certainly, certainly," replied Martin.

Hans sat, his mind filled with expectation.

It was certain that something would happen now, and he waited for it calmly. Suddenly a horizontal row of lights appeared, and a little curtained stage rose shimmering above it. A clear tinkling melody came from underneath, and the curtains faintly swayed as if set in motion by the tune. The air came to an end ; there was silence ; then another melody began, and slowly, like two butterfly wings, the curtains stirred and in semicircular folds furled themselves up and vanished.

Behind appeared a little lofty room, with black walls, a blank white window, a tiny hearth on which sparkled a fire, a table piled with books, and a wooden stool. On the stool sat a little figure with white hair and beard, in a black gown falling in stiff folds and reaching to its feet. Looking at it again Hans thought its posture had changed. A moment later he saw that it was moving. Stiffly it raised one hand above its head, and as if continuing the movement, like a form gradually coming to life, it arose and stood facing him. Slowly, by minute degrees, its arm sank to its side again, it quivered for a second, and still slowly, as if in a trance, began to walk,

THE MARIONETTE

coming towards him. As it moved it seemed to alter the fire on the hearth, the table piled with books, and the stool, which now took up different positions in relation to it, receding continuously and smoothly as the figure advanced. It walked towards him, then turned and walked back again, the room advancing as it withdrew. All at once he heard its voice, distant and tiny. But he did not listen; he thought only: "It moves! It moves!" as if in moving it had set in motion something which would never cease.

The little figure stopped in his pacing and listened. There was a faint scratching at the door; he opened it; and a small black dog scampered in and lay down immediately, as if playing a part, by the fire. Waving his arms, the figure addressed a long harangue to the dog. Then both figures were stationary, the monk sitting on the stool with his back to Hans.

All at once the dog stood up and became twice its size.

"Look!" cried Hans, clutching his father's arm.

"Don't be afraid. The dog won't be able to hurt him."

But now the dog shook itself and became twice as big again, its back nearly touching the roof. Presently the little figure turned round, started back in fear, and began to say something. He spoke for a long time, but the dog only stood swaying gigantically before him. At last he seized a book and read, facing the dog. Now the beast shook with terror; its skin swelled up and sank back in stiff creases over its body; it folded itself up like an umbrella; and with a puff of flame, a little figure in red with a plumed hat stood where it had been. As if its feet were burning, smoke rose slowly from beneath this figure, clung round its legs and body, and drifted to the roof.

"That's the devil!" said Martin.

"The devil!" replied Hans in surprise.

He kept his eyes on the new figure. It, too, began to move, speaking in a deeper, hoarse tone.

The movement became more hasty, the two figures gesticulating against each other. The curtains fell, and glimmered for a moment; then the lights went out.

"Is that all?"

"No, that's only the beginning. There's

far better to come. Do you know the story?"

"The story? Is there a story?"

"Yes. That marionette in black is Faust, and he's just sold his soul to Mephistopheles, the devil. Mephistopheles makes him young again and he falls in love with a girl called Gretchen."

"It's wonderful!" exclaimed Hans, but he was not listening to the story.

"Look, the lights are on again."

This time Hans saw a garden with two paths running away from the front of the stage, very green hedges separating them. Faust and Gretchen were coming down one of these towards him, as if stepping into subterranean light, while the devil and another woman were receding up the other. He could see only the backs of this pair, and these, blank and dead, yet moving, looked secretive and malicious. The two figures nodded their heads close together and lifted and dropped their arms as if in animated conversation. But no sound came from them; they seemed only to be pretending to speak, as if they were mocking the second pair. On the other side Faust was talking to Gretchen, coming down the path; but as soon as he began to go away he became silent, and the chatter of the devil and Martha, both gabbling at the same time, broke in with unnatural loudness. The two pairs continued to walk round at the same distance apart, never catching up on each other; and always as they advanced they spoke, and as they receded they became silent.

"What are they doing? What does it mean?" Hans asked.

But as Martin was about to reply, Gretchen ran into a little house covered with flowers in the front corner of the stage, and Faust followed. The door closed with a tiny click; the devil and Martha ran back and stood outside nodding their heads. A few words were shouted from within, the devil said something, and the curtain dropped.

"What is it? What is he doing to her?" asked Hans in excitement.

Martin explained, relating the whole story.

But now Hans sat in anxiety, his delight in the pure, processional movement of the marionettes destroyed. These figures were no longer free, but entangled in a few tiny threads which they could not discern, even while they struggled within them. As the marionettes' numbers increased, as one after another they entered with a significant bearing, like victims voluntarily offering themselves, he felt all at once that there was a secret behind everything they did; that though they really suffered they were also only pretending to suffer, that even in yielding with despairing cries to death they were at the same time doing something else of their own will. When they appeared they seemed to be presaging some action or mystery; they lifted their stiff arms as if drawing attention to themselves; but yet they appeared to be pointing to something else, still unmanifested.

It was only during the lull of their entrance that he could see them thus. As soon as they were caught into the flood of action, they passed before him in a hasty dream. One scene stood still in the centre of this rushing procession. It was night; two squat houses, their roofs invisible, their blackened walls dimly lit, rose at the back of the stage. Mephistopheles and Faust entered; a soldier was standing motionless in the shadow of a door. Mephistopheles sang in a harsh, high voice; the soldier stepped towards him, a sword in his hand. In his bearing was the steady look of one who is resolved to harm another. He lunged with his sword at the devil, and Hans thought, terrified: He wants to kill him! But the devil struck aside the sword with his guitar, which rattled thinly against the blade, and Faust, drawing his rapier, passed it through the centre of the soldier's body. The soldier fell with a clatter, his limbs suddenly angular, and Mephistopheles and Faust ran away.

"He's dead!" cried Hans.

"Yes. He's dead," replied Martin uneasily.

Only two scenes remained, but these passed still more indistinctly before him. They seemed, after the murder of the soldier, to be concealing something behind their properties, to be covering up traces of blood which were there, though they could not be discovered. Everything was glittering and clean, but there was blood on it which could not be wiped away; blood on the walls of Gretchen's cell, in the streets, and on everybody's hands. The physical sensation of blood so obsessed him that he continued to sit in silence for several minutes after the play had finished, hardly aware of its end.

On the way home the streets passed him in a dream. He felt again that he was beneath the sky, but it was a remote, shining vacancy to him.

CHAPTER VI

WHEN Martin went up to the room that evening Hans greeted him with an absent look. He seemed to be sunk in an effort of concentration which made his face pensive and intelligent. Martin tried to discover what he had thought of the marionettes, but he only said: " They are wonderful! " and returned to his thoughts. Martin left him in a few minutes.

Now the figures which had passed in a haze before him began to separate themselves and emerge singly. They arose one by one, with a special gesture, fixed and significant, as if each were distinguishing himself from the others, and drawing attention to himself. They arose against the backgrounds in which he had seen them. They were in cells, rooms, and small, enclosed gardens, very green. He saw everything in the cell, the room, the garden, which seemed to awaken and become more watchful because only one figure stood in it. These scenes were very small, packed as if in a fold of the earth underground, and more vivid than the upper world. The gardens were greener; the lighted rooms glowed like lamps; the scarlet, yellow, and purple robes shone out as if irradiated from within. The marionettes' faces, fixed in a changeless resolution, gave their actions something fatal and absolute. The tension of their wills would never relax until they fell, angular and rebellious, in death.

Gradually this world, terrible at first, became conceivable and even familiar to him. He had not seen more than a dozen figures, but it seemed to him that he had beheld a multitude. Closed in till now by fear of everything, his mind opened and was peopled by these. He had seen dreadful things happen to them; he had shared their fear; but now he was not afraid. Terrors other than his own had entered his mind and passed through it; those who had incarnated them remained behind as fixed forms, their agony spent, leaving, by their number and the gestures which separated and yet wove them together, the image of a world.

For several nights he dreamed of marionettes. On a little black hill which seemed to be underground he saw a marionette army standing, the figures very tiny, and clad in scarlet from head to foot. Below was a burnt plain where was ranged a second horde, all in black, taller, with long, spiny lances waving like antennæ. All at once, with expressionless faces and stiff, clumsy limbs, the two armies rushed against each other. They fought silently in a straight line until all were fallen, the dead warriors lying stiff on their backs with their faces staring upwards. Hans looked towards the hill again. The dead armies were vanished, but on the hill a multitude, their backs towards him, stood gazing at something farther away which he could not discern. The light dimmed; the hill was now a black hump; and the crowds standing upon it bristled black against a sky, white as paper, which gave no light. Through the pale sky fell slanting, with a tearing sound, a ball of yellow fire; and from the crowd floated a sound of distant lamentation. Through Hans's mind flashed the words: "The end of the world."

Another time he dreamed he was in a town with many domes, and houses the colour of tarnished gold. This town, also, was underground, and the dark brown air, permeated by the scent of old spices crumbled to dust, quivered with the deep, golden jangling of bells. The streets were thronged with stationary multitudes, their faces lifted to the sky. Hans saw Mephistopheles standing among them, and Gretchen near by in the dress she had worn in prison. They all lifted their arms slowly in solemn rejoicing, their faces turned immovably aloft.

There was one dream which terrified him. It recurred persistently, was very brief, and more like a picture than a dream. Close by on his right hand arose a squat pillar crowned by a little platform with a smooth, circular stone balustrade. This pillar stood beside a magnificent and very large palace, but the palace he could never see. Leaning from the balustrade was an old, ugly woman, a marionette. She was looking at two soldiers; one standing beneath her, with implacable, stripped limbs, like a Roman soldier; the other a little distance away at the foot of a flight of stairs, his body strangely frail. This second marionette filled Hans with loathing and fear. His body was soft, as if made of wool; his face pale, like kneaded dough; his legs, of a hard metal, were slender and spidery. In one hand he held a long spear, thin as a needle, and deadly. The old woman nodded to the Roman soldier and whispered: "Kill it! Kill it!" and the Roman soldier rushed against the other furiously, swinging his sword. But on its thin, ugly legs the other ran away very fast, and turning, flung his spear at the pursuer. The spear passed clean through his body and he fell dead. Hans knew that the second soldier was one of a new race of marionettes, who would destroy the old, and afterwards each other.

This dream troubled him; he saw the marionettes living in the shadow of destruction. Yet this made their existence more intense. He saw their underground city sunk in a solid chasm of light and heat, which did not issue from the sun, but from a gigantic, circular stone, like a flashing eye, clamped midway in the vault of black rock which was their firmament. Its rays were so strong that they pierced through walls and roofs, and as he looked at the houses all the rooms were visible. These rooms, stretching in rows, piled in tiers, were filled with marionettes; long rooms in which many of them, in a single line, danced and yet were stationary, like figures on a frieze; others in which they stood motionless in a group, all gazing in the same direction; still others in which they sat in rows, suddenly turning their heads in unison, as if looking at something he could not see. Before them, in the streets, passed other marionettes who did not perceive them, though the walls were transparent. These seemed to be clothed in heat, and walked on flagstones which sealed furnace fires; their limbs were clear and polished, like those of creatures which live in flame. The little black hills showing over the roofs gleamed smoothly, like steel. When night came the light was shut off like an eye closing, the firmament became white as paper, and as it faded the blackness was like ebony. Then the rooms along the street glowed like lighted lanterns, and within them, stretching in lines which disappeared far away, tier above tier, in multitudes, the marionettes showed themselves to the night.

At this hour a change came over the marionettes. The tension of their limbs relaxed, their rigid forms awoke to a second life. They danced, walked to and fro, were happy and unhappy, laughed and wrung their hands, as he had seen them doing on the stage. Faust and Mephistopheles, Gretchen and Martha, appeared always at this hour; during the day, when all the marionettes had the same form, they could not be discerned. He saw them sitting together in a room, their faces serene; then in separation, the light mysteriously fallen from them. Other scenes appeared, with figures unknown to him. In the topmost nook of a lofty row of buildings he watched, in a little chamber suffused with rosy light and filled with flowers, a love-scene. The illuminated rooms on every side secluded this room and made it private; and the two figures were in a hidden world as they advanced towards each other and delicately, with a secret thrill which Hans could feel, their finger-tips met. During the day his mind lingered on this scene; he saw again all the figures he had beheld in the theatre; but his dreams were of the other marionette world: the fiery streets, the iron hills, the mechanical race bound on secret business.

With his father he went every evening to the top of the Kapuziner Berg. But the trees widely spaced, the broad, easy paths, the landscape in which a house appeared only here and there, the comfortable town beneath him, the ineffectual blue sky, the diffused light, a vacant radiance in the air, the fields all of the same innocent green, the black mountains, too vast and awkward in their strength, seemed inane and clumsy after the marionette world. He felt friendly towards them now; they did not terrify him any longer.

Martin took him to the theatre again. They saw a farce describing the adventures of Kasperl, a red-nosed rascal dressed in Tyrolese costume, who played tricks on the fat mayor, knocked Sepp, the policeman, on the head, and came away scot-free. Hans continually asked questions, took sides, and near the end became jealous of Kasperl. As they walked home he said suddenly: " That was silly ! "

" You didn't like it ? " asked Martin in surprise. " You didn't think it funny ? "

" No. It wasn't funny. Why was the policeman so stupid ? He could have caught Kasperl if he hadn't been looking the other way."

They saw several plays in the next few weeks: melodramas, fairy plays, comedies in which

Kasperl was always the chief actor, and "Faust" in another version.

As Hans saw more of the marionettes his world of fantasy changed; the figures became individualised. The race, all alike, peopling the streets, inhabiting the rooms all day, and coming to a separate existence at night, melted away. He recognised the different figures now; he liked some, and disliked others. He knew the streets where they walked, and was familiar with the crossings, the squares, the churches, and certain of the houses. Over one row of buildings the shadow fell always, solid and stationary; another lay perpetually in brilliant light. There was a vacant square surrounded by gigantic, blank palaces, doorless and windowless, where no figure ever appeared, and the light dwelt by itself. There was a street continually thronged by two equal crowds passing in opposite directions. The doors and windows were always sealed, but another multitude, parted by interior walls and ceilings, sat or stood in the rooms, divided as by a wall of silence from those outside. But always, in a house, or among the crowds in the street, Hans recognised a figure he knew.

THE MARIONETTE

The marionette he loved most was Gretchen. When she appeared on the stage, her glassy eyes melting with meaningless love, he felt that she was gazing at him. As she lifted her arm and pointed, she seemed to be beckoning towards a place where they would be together, away from everyone; and the thought of being alone with her filled him with mingled delight and terror. Faust, Mephistopheles, Valentine, her brother, were always round her; she could not escape from them: but it was him that she loved, and all her glances, which they could not entice away, were his. He saw her in the garden walking with Faust; in the prison cell, the fetters clamped round her ankle. But she seemed to be saying that she wore the pearls for him, that she stood apart in the glade that he might come, and that when the prison was opened and she was set free, then she would be his for ever. Through all those scenes she seemed to be waiting for this, her eyes fixed on him to give her strength. He carried her image with him all day, but he did not speak of her to Martin.

In the shed, where he now spent the warm spring days, he enacted parts. He was Valentine and fought with the devil, but was not vanquished. He was an imaginary character who appeared when Kasperl thought he was triumphant, seized the handcuffs which Sepp always dangled helplessly by his side, and clapped them on. But generally he dramatised himself. In his own person he appeared among the marionettes, commanded Faust, Mephistopheles, and Valentine to leave the country, and, opening the door of the prison, led Gretchen away by the hand over a long road which took them to a valley where there was a green-and-white house.

CHAPTER VII

HANS's entry into the marionette world changed it for him. He no longer watched it from without. Like the others he exercised power, but his power, he discovered, was not infinite. When he punished Kasperl, disappointment followed his triumph; Kasperl remained Kasperl still, his nature unchanged. In his mind Hans could do what he liked to the marionettes; he could pull them asunder, cut up their limbs, and burn the pieces; but then, as he was preparing to enjoy his victory, there was something more that he had to do, and he had to begin perpetually again.

Yet action now filled his days and made him happier than he had ever been before. He felt capable and free. Two things never came into his world. The marionettes did not bear children, nor did they die. He had seen them fall dead on the stage; in his dreams they had lain in heaps on the fields;

but they were not really dead, and there were no funeral processions through the streets. They loved, were jealous, quarrelled, fought over their possessions, or because they hated each other. In these things was their life.

He had tried to make his dolls move and speak like the marionettes. But they sat dumb and stupid all day, and when he compelled one of them to walk a few steps and let it go, it fell on its back, its eyes staring at the ceiling, one arm awkwardly stuck upwards, the other by its side. He tried all three of them, one after the other. They lay for awhile in the shed as they had fallen. After a few days he flung them under the bench, out of sight.

To Martin he seemed greatly changed. On his walks on the Kapuziner Berg he talked continuously, and sometimes he sought out his father in the study to tell him something that had happened. His conversation was all about the marionettes. Every evening he related the happenings of the day, asking Martin whether, in such and such a case, he had done rightly. Martin was astonished by his intelligence. The marionettes, he thought, might be a means of leading him into the actual world. If he could show so much sense in ordering an imaginary life, why should he not show it in the real world as well? Sometimes Martin tried to lead the conversation from the one world to the other, saying: "The very same thing happened to a man in Salzburg last week," or: "That was very like Herr Meyerbold. Have you ever heard of him?" But always Hans stopped displeased, and would not go on.

Martin saw Hans more often now. Sometimes he would neglect his book for a morning to listen to his stories. He asked questions, trying to make the actions of the characters comprehensible. He would say: "Why did Faust do this?" or: "How did Mephistopheles happen to be there?" But Hans had always a good reason. Though everything in the marionette world was clear and childish, though no animals were in it, and neither birth nor death, it seemed to be as consistent as the real one. It existed, a reduplication of the actual world, and as he felt its completeness, it seemed to Martin that existing thus, in rivalry, it made the existence of the actual world more arbitrary. It was not shadowy, like the worlds of imagination and religion, but created solidly like Salzburg or Vienna;

there was no room in it for mystery. Every day while he listened to Hans he was taken farther into it. He felt sometimes that this was foolish, that it was even dangerous; but he could not stop.

Emma seldom spoke to Hans now. The intimacy between him and Martin had at first made her uneasy; at present it filled her with exasperation. Both had changed since the day when she had brought them together; there was something happening between them which she could not understand, and this, whatever it was, was wrong. She had only wanted Martin to acknowledge Hans's presence in the house, to treat him humanely as a poor half-wit and his son; but now they talked together all day about things which did not exist. Hans with his new self-confident bearing and shining face exasperated her. Sometime he would awaken, and then what would happen? It would have been better if his father had left him alone. Martin too had changed. He rarely went to the café or to see his friends; he often gave up at a trifling excuse his morning's work, which he had not missed for years; he even dressed more carelessly. She came upon them in the passages, in the rooms, so deep in conversation that they did not see her as she passed. "It's like a mad house!" she exclaimed to herself when she reached her room. But she went on cooking the meals, tidying the rooms, and waiting for the disaster which must come. They might need her then.

Once Hans began to tell her about the marionettes. But she would not listen.

"That's all nonsense, Master Hans. You know it's nonsense."

"But it isn't nonsense, Emma. It's true."

"It's lies. I'm surprised your father listens to them. I won't."

"It isn't lies! You mustn't say it's lies! If you saw, Emma, you would believe."

"I don't want to see. There's nothing to see."

"There is something to see!" cried Hans. "Why do you say such things?"

In Emma's unbelief he felt an animosity towards the marionette world; by denying it she sought to injure it.

"She shall see it!" he exclaimed, walking about his room; yet he never tried again to win her belief.

CHAPTER VIII

It was now the beginning of May. The marionette theatre was closed, but Herr Hoffmann announced that he would give one more performance for Hans.

"Which play would you like to see?" asked Martin. "You're to have your choice, seeing that this is the last one."

"The last one? There will be no more at all?"

"Not for a long time. Not till winter. You'll see new ones then, that you've never seen before. All summer Herr Hoffmann prepares them. He's very busy and has to think of them all the time."

"How does he prepare them? What does he do?"

"I don't know! I don't know!" replied Martin. He did not want to tell Hans that the marionettes were made in Herr Hoffmann's workshop behind the stage. "It's a secret."

"And then, when Herr Hoffmann has done

this," said Hans, "there will be other marionettes there next winter?"

"Yes. But now you must decide which play you want to see. Remember, it will be a long time before you see it again, so choose the one you like best."

"Then I should like to see 'Faust,'" replied Hans.

He wanted only to see "Faust," and that he was to see it once more seemed very important and yet in a sense not to matter.

As he set out with his father, his last journey down the hill seemed different from the others. The figures on the stations of the Cross were remote in meditation, as if they were not seeing him but the fate which made this his last pilgrimage past them. The slanting light lay serenely on the smooth-painted figures on the squares of wood; evenly, like a still sunset river, the blood flowed from the Saviour's side; their eyes fixed on Christ as if through all time pitying and shielding Him, the Roman soldiers stood, their iron helmets heavy and smooth above their tranquil faces. Christ gazed on, peacefully smiling, the blood flowing quietly from His side, the plaited thorns pricking His untroubled brow, the smooth-planed Cross holding Him motionlessly suspended, as if standing in the air. Hans's passing recalled to Him and His executioners the scene in which they had been waiting in a stationary trance; they seemed to be contemplating themselves from a distance as they gazed at Hans walking down the hill. The sky above them was vaster, the mountains far away over the towers of Salzburg and the plain came near, grew and rose, as if they were gathering round the little path winding down the hill.

The buildings along the street seemed to make way for him to-day. Strangers on the pavement gazed at him for a moment before they passed, as if they knew that this was his last journey to the theatre, and were sorry for him. Herr Hoffmann greeted him with respect. He led him to a seat in the third row, and before he turned to go to the back of the stage said: "We'll do our best to-day."

Hans did not want to talk, and Martin sat in silence, without moving, by his side. Brilliantly, not as if for the last time, the horizontal row of lights sprang out of the dusk at the end of the hall; the stage curtains rose

THE MARIONETTE

above it shimmering, as if repeating something which always, at a certain moment, would be repeated. The automatic, tinkling melody arose, the curtains swayed, the tune came to an end. Then, after a pause, as if starting a new movement, another air began, the curtains stirred, and smoothly, like a butterfly slowly furling its wings, ascended in two equal semicircles and vanished.

Behind appeared the cell. The stool, the table piled with books were there; the fire sparkled, tiny and inconquerable, on the hearth. Faust sat as he had done the first time, motionless as the table and the stool, a part of the chamber which, like them, would be there always. But when he lifted his arms and arose, everything was changed. On the stage, as on an indifferent shore from which a ship was receding, he walked, occupied by his own affairs, taking part in an action which would continue when Hans was not there to see. The dog scampered in and lay down by the fire. Mephistopheles appeared, his gestures perfunctory and mocking; but he would be the same to-morrow and the next day; he would go on always doing what he was doing now.

But when, after the pause, Gretchen came walking down the path between the green hedges, Faust by her side, Hans felt: " I shall never see her again." Faust, Mephistopheles, the cell, the garden, would remain; but she would not be there. As she entered, her eyes were fixed on him; but when she lifted her arm it was in farewell. The garden glittered bright green, as it had done before, when, past the importunity of Faust, she had gazed at him full of love. Now it was like part of another scene, where other figures hid and waited to enact a different drama which he did not know. It glittered, vivid and malignant, then faded as he gazed at Gretchen. She seemed to become taller; her eyes, grown large and brilliant, held him; something was happening; and involuntarily he pressed back against his chair. He did not desire this to happen, and he tried by looking intently at Gretchen to make her return to her former shape.

Presently the green hedges grew round her again, solid and stationary to the last swordpointed leaf, and she was a marionette like Faust and Mephistopheles. She remained a marionette while she knelt beside the shrine praying to the Virgin and sat in the church listening to the litany of the choir. But in the prison cell in the last scene, when Faust entered, she changed again. When, ignoring Faust and singing her insane song, she came to the front of the stage as if commanded to show herself to the whole world, she floated out and hung full in his gaze. This happened once more without warning; he tried again to make her return to her former shape, but this time she remained suspended outside the stage. Then something happened. He heard a sharp, breaking noise, which seemed to come from somewhere else; the image of Gretchen trembled and fell, and before him, a few feet away, the stage was in disorder. Gretchen, now a small puppet, was lying awkwardly on her back; there was something strange in her posture; he could see only one of her feet. Then he saw the other, fettered to a chain which was clamped into the wall of the cell. This foot, neatly broken off above the ankle, lay in a clear space near the front of the stage. He leapt up, but Martin laid a hand on his shoulder and forced him down again.

"Don't be afraid," he said. "The leg can be mended."

The curtains dropped hurriedly; there was a secretive bustle behind the stage; the lights remained on.

"It's all wrong!" cried Hans. "That should not be in the play!"

"Never mind!" replied Martin.

"But it's wrong!" Hans repeated. "It shouldn't have happened. It should not be in the play, should it?" he asked, turning to Martin.

"No; it was an accident. But it can be put right."

"It shouldn't have happened at all," persisted Hans. He chafed in his seat, but did not rise again. The stage seemed far away, and he was helpless.

Herr Hoffmann came towards them.

"I'm very sorry," he began. "But it was almost the end of the play, after all. I moved Gretchen too hastily; I had forgotten about the chain round her leg. I can't imagine how I was so stupid."

After Hoffmann had hurried away, Hans remained sitting. Martin touched his arm, but he sat still, his fingers clutching the arm of the chair. The bustle behind the stage sank into silence; only the lights remained on;

THE MARIONETTE

at last, with a tiny click, these vanished, and the hall was completely dark.

"Come! We must go now," cried Martin, "or we'll be locked in!"

Hans rose. As he walked out he gazed stubbornly at the point where the stage had appeared. But the stage had vanished and he would never find it. He did not know where Gretchen was; somewhere behind the stage, past one wall, and then another, and then another, in darkness through which as through a maze he would stumble and never find her. He dared not penetrate there, and he followed his father to the door, through the little archway and out into the street. He walked slowly, as if his feet were keeping him near the theatre. When the houses were behind and, surprised that he was there already, he found himself passing the stations of the Cross, he realised at last that he would never see Gretchen again, and now instead of lagging he began to walk fast.

CHAPTER IX

EMMA was in the hall when Martin and Hans returned. She looked at them and saw that something had happened. Hans ran up the stairs, and Martin, with a hasty nod, hung up his hat and went into the study.

He sat down dejectedly; all that he had tried to do had been ruined by this accident. He wondered what Hans was thinking of the marionettes now; probably this had destroyed his trust in them, and he would have nothing more to do with them. The breaking of the marionette's ankle must have shocked him as a real accident in a play would shock the spectators; for instance, if an actor were to have a stroke or were to fall dead. It was the breaking in of something that was forgotten for the time, and it would call up images of all the other perils which lay beyond the protected stage. When something real and horrible happened there it must seem more threatening, as if it were close to you. Yes, Hans would probably set himself to forget the marionettes after this. In that case, Martin thought, I shall have to begin again; but how? and he could think of nothing which would do for Hans what the marionettes had done. He wondered if there was no way of repairing the damage. If he were to bring Gretchen here, after her leg had been mended, and give her to Hans?

There was a knock at the door and Emma entered.

"What has happened to Hans?" she asked. "He's been crying ever since he came in. He won't tell me anything."

"He'll get better," replied Martin. "Something unexpected happened at the marionette theatre when we were there."

"I thought it was the puppets. I've been expecting this, Herr Scheffer."

"You don't understand, Emma," replied Martin. "I can't explain at present, but this is a stage that he has to pass through."

"I don't agree with Herr Scheffer. See where 'the stage' has brought him."

"I assure you, Emma, I've thought it out. You must take it on trust for the present. And don't be against me. I'm doing the best I can for him."

"Herr Scheffer must act as he decides," replied Emma coldly. "Hans is in his room."

Martin wondered again what was the best thing to do. Should he tell Hans that the world of marionettes was an illusion and that the real world was Salzburg? No, he could not do that; Hans would not understand him, and it would make things worse.

Presently he went upstairs, stood for a moment listening outside Hans's room, and, hearing nothing, turned the door-handle. The room was empty. He must have gone down to the shed, thought Martin, and he went downstairs again.

As he neared the shed he heard an irregular banging noise. Turning aside, he looked in through the window. Hans was walking from end to end of the shed, swinging a doll by the head. When he reached the wall he lifted it and smashed its feet against the wood, crying, "There you are!" Then he turned, marched to the other wall, and beat the doll against it. At last he stopped in the middle of the floor and looked at the doll. Both its feet were gone, one broken off above the ankle, the other at the knee-joint. "There you are!" he cried, tossing the doll across the shed, and he began to toss about the other dolls as well. The oldest one, Fritz, had lost both arms and both legs, Karl had one leg complete except for the foot, the third doll had come off best.

Martin opened the door and went in.

"Hans," he said, "what are you doing?"

Hans stopped and looked at him.

"Come! There's no reason to carry on like this," continued Martin.

Hans held one of the dolls in his hand; he lifted it up as if to throw it, then let it fall on the floor.

"That's better," said Martin.

After a silence he began: "I know of something that will please you. It's about Gretchen."

Turning his back, Hans mumbled: "I don't want to hear about her."

"But it's good news. She's all right again. She hasn't been hurt at all."

There was no reply.

"You don't believe me?" persisted Martin. "But I can prove it. What would you say if I brought her here and showed her to you?"

Still looking the other way, Hans muttered: "I saw it all. What's the good of talking about it?"

"But I don't say that it didn't happen. I only say that Gretchen is all right again. Don't you believe me?"

"All right," replied Hans impatiently. He wanted his father to stop talking.

"Well, then, shall I bring her to you so that you can see for yourself?"

"If you like. Yes."

Hans picked up the dolls and began to fling them under the bench in the corner.

"Now you should go up to your room and wash," said Martin. "You're in an awful mess, you know."

Martin went down to the theatre. After listening to his explanation, Hoffmann gave him the marionette.

"I've glued the leg on," he said, "but she won't be of any further use to me. You'll have to be careful for a few hours not to knock her foot against anything. Wait a minute! She has her box to lie in."

He took down from a shelf a box painted bright yellow and green, and marked on the end with the name "Gretchen." Opening it,

THE MARIONETTE

he laid the marionette inside. The box was lined with cotton-wool.

When Martin returned to the house he left the box on the bench in the shed, opened the lid, and went up to Hans's room.

" I've good news for you," he said. " Come downstairs."

" What is it ? " asked Hans, getting up.

" Come and see."

They went downstairs and across the garden. Martin paused before the door of the shed, then threw it open.

" Go inside," he said, remaining by the door and signing to Hans to enter.

Hans went in and stood looking at the yellow-and-green oblong box. The sunset light fell full upon it. Gretchen, in white, lay on the billow of fleecy wool, her cheeks transparently glowing as if with fever, her hair, flooded with light, standing in stiff golden waves round her face. It had not been a lie after all, thought Hans; yet he could hardly believe that what he saw was real. While he looked the box would vanish; the part of the bench where it stood would be empty, a length of rough wood veiled with small grains of dust. He seemed to see through the box and

Gretchen lying in it this strip of blackened wood, and as he looked at it the bench, the shed, the house, the trees and rocks he had loved, everything he could remember, seemed dusty and old. He closed his eyes; he could not bear to look any longer at the box, knowing that it would vanish. He opened them again; it was still there, and Gretchen lay in it as she had done before. He advanced one foot, then the other, and stood nearer. The box remained on the bench.

"Yes, it is Gretchen," said Martin. "It is really Gretchen."

Hans walked forward and stood looking down at the marionette. Brought near like this she was different, and a new misgiving took hold of him. She seemed to be Gretchen; yet she was not the Gretchen he knew. Her eyebrows sweeping in two smooth curves seemed bold and hard; her nose, her mouth, her chin, were cruelly palpable and final; her eyes were too close to him, and after a glance at them he turned his head aside. As if they were separate arcs and spheres woven into glass he saw the blue iris and small black pupil, open and still, like the works of a machine at rest; the cheeks exactly and too deliberately tinted; the

mouth firm, physical, and without mystery;
and seeing these he could see nothing behind
them; the Gretchen he had known was not
there, in these physical lineaments. Remembering his former image of her, he felt ashamed;
he wished to cover her face, too naked and too
close to him. He turned to Martin.

"This is Gretchen? You're sure?"

"I'm certain of it. Look, that is where her
leg was broken," and walking forward Martin
lifted the hem of the gown and pointed to
the small, fretted line, like a thread, above the
marionette's ankle. Hans gazed at the foot
and nodded.

"It is Gretchen."

As soon as he pronounced her name openly
before his father, Hans was sure that it was
really Gretchen.

"Well, what did I tell you?" asked Martin. "You see that what I said was true?
You see that she's all right again?"

"Yes," replied Hans, staring in perplexity
at the marionette. "It is Gretchen."

"Then that's all right."

Martin left the shed and closed the door
after him. When he was outside he stood
still with his fingers clasping the handle. "I

THE MARIONETTE

wonder if I have done rightly," he wondered. He had an impulse to go into the shed again and take the marionette away. But he had closed the door and as he walked towards the house he felt: "This is final," and then in a flash: "This is the beginning of something new."

He paused before entering the house. If he went in now, Hans's fate would take a new turn. I am responsible, he thought, and yet all this is nonsense.

CHAPTER X

Hans remained in the shed standing beside the marionette. When the door closed with an almost imperceptible sound, he started. All at once he became aware of the stillness, and felt that the marionette was trying to compel him to break it. But he could think of nothing to say; he wanted to escape. The shed seemed small, the roof very low; he was afraid that the door might be locked. He ran to it and fumbled with the handle. Suddenly it flew open, and the garden, the mountains, and the fading evening sky lay before him. Gradually he became aware of the railings running along the front of the garden, the tree in the corner, the worn steps before the door, every line of which he knew; he wanted to remain with them. The shed was not the same now that the marionette was lying in it. He could never be there alone after this.

While he stood it had grown dark; presently he heard a half-hour strike in the town, then another clock struck it a second time. Now that the marionette could hardly be seen, he felt he must look at her again to make sure if she was really Gretchen. In the dusk he saw a pale outline in the box. He could not make out the marionette's features, and he put down his hand where he thought her face was. His fingers encountered her nose and her brow; they were unexpectedly hard, smooth, and cold. "She's just like the dolls," he thought, very much surprised. He shifted his fingers and touched her hair: it was unsubstantial, yet dry and resilient, like Karl's. "It's not Gretchen at all," he thought.

Steps sounded outside, and Martin appeared in the doorway.

"What! are you here still?" he asked. "It's quite dark! What are you doing?"

He peered into the shed, trying to distinguish Hans.

"Oh, you're there! I didn't know what had become of you. Come, it's time we went into the house."

"All right," said Hans, coming forward.

"But do you intend to leave Gretchen here?" asked Martin in surprise.

"Yes, I suppose so."

"What? Wouldn't you like to take her up to your room?"

Hans did not reply for a moment.

"I don't know. Won't she be all right here?"

"Yes, of course. But I thought you would want to have her with you."

Hans was silent.

"I'll take her," he said.

Hans closed the lid and lifted the box, which was heavier than he had expected. When he reached the room he set it down on the table in the middle of the floor. Now that it was there he wished he had not brought it. Very bright and new, it changed the appearance of the room; it seemed to intrude itself; it troubled him. Presently Martin said good night and left.

Hans stood listening to his father's footsteps. They grew faint, a door opened and shut, and the house was still. Alone in the room with the marionette, he felt uneasy again. He looked round, crossed to the door to see that it was shut, then went over to the window and drew closer the curtains. For a moment he stood holding the curtains together in his hands, his back to the room, then turned and went up to the box.

In the candle-light the marionette looked more like Gretchen than she had done in the shed. But he could never know; this might not be her, but only something very like her. On the stage she had moved and spoken; but since coming to the house she had not stirred; she was as lifeless as one of his dolls. Perhaps a trick had been played upon him. But he could not understand how it had been done, or where the deception had come in. I am sure she can't walk, he thought, as he lifted her out of the box and set her on her feet. Her legs doubled up under her and she fell on her back, as he had expected. Yet lying there now she looked exactly as Gretchen had done when she fell on the stage after her ankle had been broken. The accident seemed to have repeated itself under his eyes, and it brought before him again the scene on the stage. "It should never have happened," he said aloud. Had it really happened? He looked at the ankle of the marionette and saw the line where it had been broken. It was as if a doll exactly like Gretchen had had its ankle broken in exactly the same place. Suddenly he was certain that this had happened at the same time as well. What would that mean? Even if this was not Gretchen but only a doll, there seemed to be a connection between it and her. Or could it be Gretchen and yet not Gretchen? Would it change sometime into Gretchen if he waited, or if something he did not know of were to happen?

He laid the marionette back in the box. Feeling her wooden limbs, he thought, No, she's only a doll. His father had tried to deceive him.

In anger he shut the lid of the box.

CHAPTER XI

For several days Martin was puzzled. Whenever he went up to the bedroom Hans met him with a suspicious stare and remained standing as if waiting until he should go away. Hans's appearance had changed; he had put on a new black suit which he had refused to wear before, his face and hands were always clean, and his hair carefully brushed. About the marionette he would not say much; when he mentioned her it was never as Gretchen, but sometimes as "she" and at other times as "it."

One day Martin could see the marionette nowhere, and Hans walked about as if enjoying a joke. The three tattered dolls were lying on the table of the room when Martin went up; and Hans began to talk about them at once with simulated eagerness. He lifted them and set them upright on the stumps where their feet had been.

"See, they can't walk," he said. Then he

paused, and added casually : " The marionettes can all walk."

" So that's it," thought Martin.

"Well, that depends," he replied. " The marionettes can walk when Herr Hoffmann has them on the stage ; but otherwise they can't."

" Oh, I see," replied Hans, taken aback. He paused. Then he said, as if propounding a difficult question : " But when they're here, are they just the same as when they're on the stage ? "

" They're just the same."

Hans smiled incredulously. " But when they're on the stage they move about, and when they're not, they lie still just like Fritz there."

" All the same, if they were on the stage they could walk. Gretchen could if she were there. By the by, where is she ? "

" Oh, she's all right."

Hans held up Fritz as if inviting Martin's inspection.

" I suppose he could walk too if he were put on the stage ? "

" No, you're quite wrong. Fritz would just remain as he is now. He's only a doll."

"Is that the difference?"

"Yes, he's a doll, and Gretchen's a marionette."

"That's it, of course," assented Hans, appearing to be convinced. He said nothing more.

After leaving Hans, Martin went down to the shed to see if the marionette was there. He could not find her at first, but at last perceived the end of the box sticking out from under the bench. It had been pushed into the corner where the dolls had lain. Martin picked it up and looked inside; Gretchen was there. He returned the box to its place.

Next day the marionette reappeared in Hans's bedroom. When Martin went in, Hans was trying to make her walk on the table. On hearing the door open he took his hands away, the marionette fell, and he threw her into the box, standing between her and his father. Martin pretended not to have seen anything, and after a while began to speak again of the difference between dolls and marionettes. But Hans did not reply.

The conversation the day before had disquieted Martin; he was afraid lest Hans should be beginning to doubt the reality of the marionettes. If he were to do that the whole plan would have failed; and by this time the plan had become very important to Martin. Hans's response to the marionette appeared perverse to him now. He was resolved to impose her upon him, even if it had to be done against his will.

One day he thought: "If I were to get a suit like Faust's made for him?" But the idea seemed fantastic; he could not understand how he had come to think of it. Soon it began to appear more reasonable. If Hans were dressed like a marionette, Gretchen would begin to become real to him again; he would live the part and be done with it, and then he might be able to face the world.

Martin desired now simply to see Hans in marionette clothes. He believed that this in itself would change him, and that after he had worn the suit he would be as much better again as he had been after first seeing the marionettes.

He asked Hans one day if he would like a suit like Faust's. At first Hans thought his father was joking, but when he understood that the suit could be made he began to ask: "When can I have it?"

Martin said that he could not have it for a week at least. Frau Tuchner would have to take the measurements first, and then the suit would have to be prepared.

During the time that the suit was being made the marionette was neglected; the dolls were thrown under the bench again. Hans would ask his father; "How is it getting on now?" and every day that passed before the suit could be ready seemed to add to its mystery. He did not know what was being done during this time, but at the end of it the suit would be there complete, as if it had come into existence instantaneously. It was the only one of its kind, it was intended for him, and this made him feel that he had been singled out.

Martin entered the bedroom one afternoon with a brown cardboard box and a smaller paper parcel.

"Here it is!" he said.

Not daring to come too near, Hans looked on as Martin cut the string and lifted the lid. A parcel wrapped in tissue paper lay in the box; the paper was undone, and a plum-coloured coat rested in its folds. It dangled as Martin held it up. Around the neck was a white ruff; a fringe of lace fell from the sleeve cuffs; but what caught Hans's eyes was a row of large golden buttons running down the front; he had never seen such large buttons before. When Martin lifted up the knee-breeches Hans saw that a row of smaller golden buttons ran down each leg; and the repetition seemed to him like something he had seen in a dream.

"There you are!" said Martin. "But wait a minute."

He undid the paper parcel and took out a pair of plum-coloured stockings, and shoes adorned by large yellow buckles, still bigger than the buttons on the coat.

The parts of the suit lay scattered over the bed. At last Hans touched the coat and asked, "I can put it on?"

"Of course! Would you like to put it on now? I'll be back in a minute."

Martin waited impatiently in his room. He wanted to know at once how Hans looked in the suit. At last he went up. Hans was walking about, moving his arms and legs stiffly. The suit made him appear very tall and broad; his shoulders looked powerful, outlined by the tight jacket; his sturdy calves seemed to be bursting through his stockings; the cuffs at his wrist looked fragile and useless as they drooped about his red knuckles. "He's as big as a man. He's stronger than I am," thought Martin.

"Well, how do you like it?" he asked.

"It's tight. But I like it."

Above the high white ruff rising out of the plum-coloured coat Hans's face looked as it had always done. Up to the neck he was changed, but his face, stupid and perplexed, seemed to be stubbornly reiterating that this alteration had nothing to do with it. As he looked, Martin was suddenly ashamed; it was as if he had inadvertently exposed Hans's weakness, or had dressed him up for sport. Hans seemed unconscious of the absurdity of his appearance. He glanced at his father and asked: "Does it look nice?"

"Yes! Yes!" replied Martin. "It's very nice. It's quite beautiful."

He spoke kindly, as if comforting Hans for a sorrow of which he did not know.

"Wait a minute," he said. He pulled the coat straight, and made the ruff lie more evenly. But nothing could alter the suit, and as Hans bent his head to glance at his shoes he looked like an unconscious victim dressed up for a sacrifice.

"I don't think you should wear it much," Martin said. "When you want to play, put it on, but it would be best to wear your other suit for the rest of the time."

Hans paid no attention. He was walking backwards and forwards before the mirror, his lips compressed, his back held very straight.

As soon as his father left he threw up his arms in relief and began to strut as if he saw himself on the stage. He lifted his arm in an attitude before the mirror. The gesture was so splendid that he felt he wanted to say something, but he could not think of anything to say. He turned his back on the mirror and smiled at himself over his shoulder. This was not so successful; his face remained the same as it had been when he used to stand before the glass hoping that he could alter it. But the lifting up of one arm changed everything; he had never known before that he could look like that. He tried one attitude after another. Presently he remembered Emma.

Hurrying downstairs he flung open the door of the kitchen.

"Look, Emma! Look at my suit!" he

THE MARIONETTE

exclaimed, and he began to strike his attitudes rapidly, one after another.

Emma stared at him. When he stopped he saw her face and stood still.

"Don't you like it?" he asked.

"Like it?" replied Emma slowly. "Well, of course, it's nice. Where did you get it?"

"Father gave it me."

"What next?" muttered Emma. She said aloud: "Well, do you know what I would do if I were you, Master Hans? I wouldn't wear it at all."

Hans stamped his foot.

"Now you've spoilt it all," he cried. "You're always trying to spoil things."

"No, no, Master Hans," Emma began; but Hans had walked rapidly away.

That day Emma packed her trunk, but at the last moment Martin persuaded her to remain. In reality she could not leave Hans in the house with his father.

CHAPTER XII

AT first the coming of the suit seemed to have estranged Martin from Hans. Both felt embarrassed, and Hans never practised his attitudes when his father was present.

He wore the suit every day. The morning after it came he began to put on his ordinary clothes: then he stopped, folded them up and laid them away in the wardrobe. During the first few days, alone in the room in his new suit, he was sometimes afraid. Certain attitudes produced as if by chance an effect he had not expected. He would raise his arm in imitation of a gesture he had seen on the stage; an attitude would take shape in the mirror; but it was not the one he had tried to produce. Another figure was there; a moment before it had been himself in a marionette suit, now it was somebody else, like him, who did not wear these clothes in play, but as his natural garb.

Generally Hans knew that he was pretending,

but when the change came the pretence passed instantaneously into an action outside himself. Looking at him from the mirror was another Hans, who seemed to be trying by signs to show him something. This other Hans must live in another house, in a distant place. Perhaps Martin knew where it was, but there were no roads which could take one there. Yet if he could reach it he knew that he himself would be this other Hans.

Whenever he became aware of his face in the mirror the figure vanished; he was in his room wearing a fancy suit; this was a day like every other day. The suit forgotten, he would stare at his face, and as if the sight of it had confronted him with an insurmountable obstacle, his limbs would feel impotent. At last he would turn away, but as he sat regarding the golden buttons and the buckles, which seemed useless now, gradually the thought of the other house and the other Hans would return. One day when he was feeling very tired he saw the house distinctly. At first he was looking at three trees set in a row, the trunks clean and smooth, every leaf glittering separately. These three trees stood by themselves; he felt that they were very important.

Presently he saw that a wall ran behind them, and shielded by this, in the corner, were rows of flowers. At first these were so faint that they seemed patterns on the surface of the stone, but slowly they detached themselves and stood separate. While he was looking at them a bench had appeared in a different part of the garden, a path ran past it to a gate, and from the gate, on either side, twisted railings, painted green, went along a wall. On the other side of the garden had appeared meantime the front of a house, with a door and steps running down from it. In a flash he saw that this was his own garden; only it was smaller and everything was clean and new. There was the tree in the corner with the trunk worn smooth by his fingers; it was so small and pretty that he had not recognised it before. The flowers were the same as those which were growing just now outside his window. The garden lay in clear light, and the tiny round of the sky above it, deep blue and cloudless, seemed to close it in and seclude it. Suddenly on the bench he became aware of two recumbent forms which had not been there before. Seated side by side, as motionless as if they were part of the bench, the lines of their brows and cheeks, half-turned away from him, were waxen and strange. The light flowed smoothly over them, seeming to make them inanimate; his heart beating, he tried to distinguish what they were, but he could not pierce their ambiguous lines. When the one farthest away slowly turned, revealing a serene face, it was as if one form had melted into another. The figure who looked round was himself, but smaller and younger, the face radiant, the eyes clear and peaceful. Presently the other figure turned his face too, so that Hans saw it. It was Martin; he also was younger. Soon both began to walk arm-in-arm up and down the garden; then they went into the house. Hans did not see them again.

While this happened, Hans knew he was sitting in his room; he could hear the fluttering of the curtains, and the cries of the town coming in through the open window. When he got up he felt that this other house was a great distance past the other side of the marionette city. Until recently he had lived in the marionette city whenever he liked, as if its existence did not depend on him. But the house he could see only in glimpses;

sometimes he could almost reach it, but never quite. His acting before the mirror in a suit like the one worn by the other Hans had revealed it first to him; certain things he did then made the other Hans come into the mirror; this was because he was doing them at the same time. But the change only lasted an instant; if he tried to prolong it by keeping his arm rigid, the other Hans vanished, he was looking at his own reflection, and the end of the bed or the back of a chair, coming into the mirror, fixed the room and the house around him.

He never spoke to his father about the other house. But his knowledge that his father lived in it along with the other Hans gave him a secret affection for him which he kept to himself. He doesn't know, he sometimes thought, looking at his father. One day he took Martin's arm and began to walk up and down the room with him. Both were embarrassed for a moment, but Hans persisted, as if he were resolved to show his father something. From this day they felt that they had become more intimate.

During the first days after the suit came Hans seemed to forget the marionette; the box remained closed. One afternoon he lifted the lid. The marionette's eyes as if just opened looked at him as they had looked at him from the stage; she was exactly like Gretchen; he was convinced now that his father had not deceived him. In his new suit he saw her differently; it seemed to be possible now that she should be Gretchen and not Gretchen at the same time. As he stood, suddenly he knew that the other Hans and the other Gretchen were gazing at each other on the stage. He thought: They are standing there at this moment. Perhaps they have met just now for the first time. What were they about to do? What was he opening his lips to say to her? But both disappeared, and he was standing in his room alone. Feeling that something momentous was happening on the stage, he went forward and took the marionette's hand. If he could say something now, he would share in what they were doing. A memory of things he had heard struggled up in his mind; he waited, but they did not come. He let Gretchen's hand fall.

After this Gretchen came into his visions of the other house. She walked about with Hans and his father in the garden; but most of the time all three sat on the bench without moving, the light flowing over their bowed, half-averted faces.

One afternoon a speech heard some time in the marionette theatre rose to his mind. When he took the marionette's hand he found himself saying:

> " And didst thou know me, sweetest angel, when
> Thou sawest me coming through the garden now ? "

He pronounced these stilted words solemnly, as if they meant something mysterious. Other words were rising in his mind, and he replied for the marionette:

> " Did you not see it ? I cast down my eyes."

The reply seemed to establish a secret between Gretchen and him whose meaning he did not know. As he stood motionless, another sentence formed itself:

> " And thou forgivest the freedom that I took ? "

These words were the most mysterious of all. He did not know what the " freedom " was; he only knew that it was something which he had done at some time, and that now he could never know what it was. He was standing in an empty street. Gretchen faced him; the sun was overhead; on either side were tall houses, with rows of vacant windows; a pavement ran up behind him to a crest crowned by a church, and in front fell steeply down to a hollow in which he saw small roofs and chimneys. A moment before he had done this act, but it had changed everything immediately, and now he could never know what it had been. The "forgive" made it more mysterious; as if Gretchen were pardoning an offence of which she did not know, or which perhaps had only been dreamt of by both of them.

These few sentences were like the beginning of something which would carry him a great distance, into places he had never imagined. Though Gretchen still lay motionless, it was as if they had set her in action in a new direction. He saw the three figures at the other house talking and laughing. They no longer sat on the bench, but walked about as if rejoicing over an event for which they had been waiting, and which had set them free.

In his father's face he seemed to see a reflection of the happiness which had come to the other house. Martin had been gratified by Hans's recent affection. The plan was succeeding, he did not know how, but he could feel it. Only Emma remained beyond the influence of the change which surrounded Hans. When he met her in any of the passages he would hurry past, avoiding her face which seemed to belong to another world, not his, that still persisted.

He could remember nothing more to say to the marionette, but he rehearsed his speeches continually. Once he tried a sentence of his own. After thinking for a while he said: "Gretchen, I love you"; but the words seemed unreal and lifeless; he knew at once that he was only Hans standing in his room in a fancy suit. But presently these words recalled others:

"Yea, my child! He loves thee!
 Oh, knowest thou what that means ? He loves thee!"

This was what he had wanted to say; now it had been said at last. "He loves thee!" he repeated, and "he" seemed to him mysterious and significant, where "I" had been unreal.

When he awoke next morning he knew that something had happened. At first he could

123

THE MARIONETTE

not recall what it was, then he saw the box on the table and remembered what he had said to Gretchen yesterday. This was the first of a new succession of mornings. They would come one after another, like the mornings in the other house where the other Hans was. "I am as happy as he is now," he thought. "I can do whatever he does."

That day he went down to the garden for the first time in his marionette's suit. He would do now whatever the other Hans did. He walked about; nobody passed; nothing happened; at last he went up to his room, carried Gretchen down, propped her on the bench, and sat down beside her. It was a sunny day; he sat for a while, trying to keep the position in which he had seen the other Hans sitting.

Martin was disquieted by Hans's appearance in the garden in his marionette suit. He tried to persuade him to remain in the room while he wore it; but Hans seemed to consider it very important that he should sit on the bench with the marionette. At last Martin ceased to expostulate.

One Saturday Hans went down to the garden early in the afternoon. It was hot and on the bench he became drowsy; at last he fell asleep, the marionette by his side. He was dreaming of the house. Gretchen and the other Hans were sitting on the bench, but they remained motionless for so long that he began to be afraid. Suddenly from the door and windows burst a clamour of yells and groans, and the two figures sprang to their feet, quivering with terror. Hans awoke. The garden appeared to be filled with noise. Voices he had never heard before seemed to be shouting at him. He leapt up; the garden was empty; the sun was beating down on his head. Suddenly above the edge of the wall he saw a row of heads.

"He's still sleeping!"

"Hi, hi! You! Wake up!"

"Look at his doll!"

Hans stood dazed and motionless, then with a quick movement picked up the marionette and clasped her in his arms, looking at the boys.

"Loony! Loony!" they began to cry.

Involuntarily clenching his fists, Hans turned his head from side to side as if not knowing where to go. He made a step towards the wall where the heads were. "Come on!" someone cried, and a stone hit him on the knuckles, making him drop his arm. He still held the marionette in the other. Emma appeared round the corner of the house. "Out of this!" she cried, walking straight towards the boys. Another stone flew past Hans, but the wall was empty.

"You'll hear about this yet," shouted Emma.

Hans ran into the house. When he reached his room the marionette was still clasped in his arms. Everything was quiet; the clamour of voices had stopped; he noticed that he was trembling; the marionette fell to the floor. He was still dazed; the row of faces and the cries were like something real and terrible which had come between two folds of sleep. It had fallen upon him when he was helpless; it had passed; now it was gone, as if it had never been. But he knew that he had not been able to guard Gretchen and himself, and he sat with his back to the marionette, too miserable to look at her. Suddenly he rose to his feet. He was recalling how he had been compelled to look at the row of faces, though he had felt that they were not really there. He had felt like that before. Where was it ? Gradually he began to remember a dream which he had once had. He stood bound hand and foot in a rocky place, and round him were armed puppets, their faces and garb strange. He searched the crevices of the rocks with his eyes, but he saw only the tall, black shadows, a motionless multitude, and behind them, far away, the low sun serenely descending. He knew that his friends, the marionettes, had deserted him and that he had been betrayed at last. As he woke the words: " Himself he could not save," were in his mind. They returned now. He caught sight of the knuckles of his left hand, stiff with dried blood. He wanted to destroy the new world which had betrayed him, but all at once he felt tired and sat down.

As he sat the house came into his mind. The other Hans and the other Gretchen were still there; this had not happened to them; they would always be secure. He was nothing to them; they had not saved him. All at once he began to take off the marionette suit. Throwing it into the bottom of the wardrobe, he took out the old suit which he had worn when he had gone through the streets and up the Gaisberg. Catching sight of the marionette he felt angry. "I don't want you here," he said, and he laid her outside the door.

When he sat down again he felt calmer. His ordeal in the garden seemed farther away, as if a change had been set between it and him. He stared at the table, the bed, the chairs; it seemed to him that he had forgotten them during these weeks; now they looked as if they had been waiting for him and this moment. Presently he began to cry, and as he cried he seemed gradually to become a former Hans whom he had forgotten. Rising up, he went over to the basin and washed his bruised knuckles; then seeing the traces of tears on his face, wiped them away. Though he felt happier now, his face, as he gazed into the mirror, seemed sadder, and he looked at it with compassion.

CHAPTER XIII

MARTIN had been out that afternoon. When he returned Emma told him what had happened. "This is what comes of dressing Hans up like a scarecrow," she concluded.

Martin went up to the bedroom. He noticed that Hans had put on his old suit, but did not dare to ask any questions. Hans spoke as if nothing had happened; but he was silent and distant, and Martin was reminded of the first evening he had gone up to see him. He could think of nothing to say, but as he rose to go he remarked: "Don't trouble about it. It's not so bad as you think." Hans pretended not to understand, gave him a distant look, and did not reply.

Martin had not seen the marionette anywhere. He went down to the shed. The box had been pushed under the bench.

Hans now became more neglectful of his appearance. He continued to wear the old suit, and would forget for days to wash his face. He never went to the garden, but Martin would find him at all hours wandering about the passages. For the greater part of the day he remained in his room. He had brought Fritz, his oldest doll, up there; the two which had been given him on his birthday remained lying under the bench in the shed, along with the marionette. Martin tried to persuade him to go for a walk on the Kapuziner Berg, but he would not leave the house.

Emma and he had become friendly again. " It was I who was there when the boys were trying to frighten him," thought Emma, and this seemed to her to have been ordained by fate. Now she seemed to know all Hans's wishes. She took away his dirty clothes and left clean ones; she reminded him to wash his face. Hans was friendly towards Martin, but he spoke to him as he might have spoken to a stranger.

After a while he began to visit the shed again. The box lay on the bench now with the lid open, and he would spend an afternoon walking about, now and then stopping to look at the marionette. Then he would not go to the shed for several days. But all at once he would seem to remember, and return.

In the afternoon when the sun lay bright and sultry in the shed, he would become restless. He would open the door and look out, then turn back and walk to and fro, casting hostile glances at the walls. Sometimes he stood for a long time with his back turned to the marionette.

One afternoon, as he was standing in a corner, he saw close to his right foot the head of one of the dolls, which had fallen sideways from its place under the bench. He had forgotten the dolls ever since he had flung them there, and for a time he stared at the head and neck lying exposed. At last he stooped down and drew the doll from beneath the bench. Its face and clothes were covered with dust and one leg dangled as he raised it. Taking out his handkerchief he began to wipe its face and hair. It was Karl, the doll with the yellow frizzy hair which Emma had given him on the first morning, before she had taken him into the study to see his father. Although it had lost a leg, its face, after the dust had been removed, looked at him, impudent and new, as if nothing had happened.

It had a stubborn expression; and suddenly furious, he seized it by the leg, swung it in the air, and brought its face down on the bench. Now its nose was broken, but as if ignoring this it still stared at him, its expression unchanged. He flung it back under the bench, kicked it in farther with his foot, and left the shed. He stayed all afternoon in his room.

One day in the shed he began to undress the marionette. The door was open; he went over and closed it. As he lifted the marionette out of the box she seemed to grow longer; her gown fell farther down, covering her feet; her hair lengthened, sliding in successive waves, till its ends, coming to rest, rippled below her waist. The gown clung about her shoulders; he jerked it loose so that it slid from her shoulders and over her arms.

Now she was naked. He laid her back in the box, and standing up stared at her, trying to see her clearly. But she danced before his eyes, which seemed to look and not to look at the same time. He saw her arms lying stiffly by her side; her legs stretching out from the trunk, with a slight, uncomfortable crook, which never straightened, at the knee;

and two strange little hills, with a hollow between, on her breast. Her face seemed unnatural joined to this body.

He continued to look, but there was nothing more to be seen. There were only the two legs, the two arms, attached to the body with wire, and the head. He touched her shoulder with his finger. Then he pulled one of the dolls from beneath the bench and began to undress it. When he had done this he laid it beside the marionette. They were exactly the same.

He drew on the marionette's clothes again and laid her in the box. After this he did not return.

CHAPTER XIV

SHORTLY after this Hans asked his father to take him to the top of the Kapuziner Berg again. They began to go there every evening now. Hans did not return to the shed after the day when he had undressed the marionette.

One day Martin asked: "Would you like to see the marionettes? The theatre is opened again."

Hans became agitated.

"The marionettes! They've begun again?"

He seemed to see the small puppets on the stage, but now they were blazing with energy which threatened him. There appeared before him, as if rising from a pit, the houses in burning light, the crowds vigilantly motionless in the rooms, and waiting with forewarned faces in the streets. For a moment the city, with the houses, the streets, and the crowds, hung spectral and motionless; then it seemed to settle with a visible jolt on its foundations. Every moment now it became more clear; and as at a word of command the crowds began to move, and the sound reached him of the trampling of feet. This ceased; the city and the crowds were gone; and he saw himself stumbling down the last rocky steps to Elser Gasse. From a remote nook of his memory something came near, and just before him he was looking into a corner in which dust and scraps of paper circulated slowly, lifted by a small, invisible gust of wind.

"No!" he said. "I don't want to see them!"

All that day he was restless. In the night he dreamt again of the soldier marionette with the soft body and the sharp, spidery legs, and he woke in the darkness in terror. Lying awake he seemed to see Gretchen on the stage, far away, walking down the path between the hedges, her hand in that of Faust. He put out his hand in the darkness to make sure that she was on the table beside his bed; then he remembered that he had left her in the shed a long time ago and had never gone back. Perhaps she had been taken away.

Next morning as soon as he was dressed he

went down to the shed. The marionette lay in the box; dust had gathered on her hair and gown. He looked in surprise at the dust; it seemed strange that it should settle on her. He carried the box up to his room.

When he had shaken the dust from the marionette and wiped her face, she was exactly as she had been before. He went over to the wardrobe and took out the marionette suit. As he looked at it the other house came into his mind, but he could not see it clearly; perhaps it was closed up, the garden empty, and the other Hans, his father and Gretchen, fled to some place where he could not find them. Knitting his brows, he tried to bring the house before him, but instead a confusion of other pictures arose. At last he was walking through a long, deserted street leading into the country. He walked fast, for he wanted to reach before sunset a small green hill which glittered a little farther away. But as he went on the street continued to stretch for the same distance before him. All the doors were open; the windows gaped, showing dropping plaster and empty rooms. Suddenly he knew that this was a remote part of the marionette city where he had never been before. He was trying to get out of it by the road leading to the house, but he could not escape from the rows of buildings.

Drops of sweat were gathering on his forehead; he looked round and saw Gretchen lying in the box. He would try once more. Taking off his clothes, he put on the marionette suit and went up to the mirror. After a moment he raised his arm; nothing happened. He tried another attitude, but he could see only his serious face looking interrogatively at him from the mirror. This face seemed to be taking no part in what his arms were doing; it was watching, and while it watched nothing could happen. He could never get away from it.

He turned and went over to the marionette.

"And didst thou know me, sweetest angel, when
    Thou sawest me coming through the garden now?"

he began, but he seemed to be forcing himself to utter the words, and his voice sounded strange, as if it belonged to somebody else. He went on:

"And thou forgivest the freedom that I took?"

but when he came to the words:

"Yea, my child! He loves thee!"

he could not utter them. He felt tired, as if he had been beating for a long time against a wall which he could not pierce. He would not try any more. There was no other house, no other Hans and Gretchen. It was the marionette that had deceived him; now he would find out how real she was.

He lifted her out of the box and pulled off her gown. The last time he had undressed her he had scarcely seen her; like a form perpetually changing she had slipped from beneath his gaze. This time he would know. But as he continued to look he could see nothing but the head, the trunk, the two arms, the two legs, and the wires binding them together. He swung her arms outwards till the joints rattled, and bent her head back so that her hair, falling straight down, touched her heels. But he knew no more than before, and he lifted the marionette by the legs and brought her down against the iron railing of the bed. The impact sent a jar up his arm, as if she had shot a poisonous current into him; he dropped her, and she fell on the bed. As she fell he heard a tinkle of wood, and on the floor he saw an arm lying, crooked at the elbow, like the severed claw of a hard-mailed creature. It seemed not to belong to Gretchen, and he stared at it as if he had created it by magic. He could not stay in the room with it, and he ran out, leaving the marionette lying on the bed.

In the garden a sunny breeze was waving the heads of the flowers; beyond the wall two ladies, one old, dressed in black, the other young, with a yellow parasol, were walking up the hill. Only the wall separated him from them, he could see the wrinkles on the old lady's face and her eyes changing as she listened to her companion; yet the two women seemed far away. He wanted to shout over to them and make them smile at him, but their eyes seemed to be avoiding him; they looked once in surprise and turned their faces away as if displeased.

He turned, walked over to the shed, went in, and closed the door. Dust lay on the bench and the dolls' house in the corner; a spider had woven a web over the top corner of the window. Dusting the chair, Hans sat down. He knew that he would do something more before the day ended; and in the shed his resolve could grow in secret, with no one to see it. This resolve seemed evil to him, but he knew, as if it were settled, that he would carry it out. The dust lying on the bench, the spider's web, grey and dry, seemed to be telling him: Here nothing matters. At last he ran across the garden and up the stairs. Opening the door of his room, he went in.

Gretchen lay on the bed where he had dropped her, it seemed now a long time ago. He noted that her arm was gone, and was filled with pity. But he could not stop. " I can't! I can't! " he said, and he lifted the marionette, laid her in the box and flung the gown over her.

Reaching the shed, he set the box on the bench and lifted up the gown. The marionette's eyes gazed at him immediately; her limbs seemed smooth and cool, knowing nothing of her face.

" Tell me! " he said, and waited for a while.

" All right, then! " he added, went to the corner, took down a box of nails and a hammer, and laid them on the bench.

THE MARIONETTE

"I must know!" he said, raising his voice, as if drawing the attention of an invisible spectator, and taking up a long nail he planted its point in the centre of the hollow between the marionette's breasts. He felt the hammer coming down. It whistled past his ear; his eye caught the arc, glittering and exact; a thrill went through his fingers holding the nail, and he took them away. The nail had gone in a little distance.

"I must know!" he said again, and after a longer pause struck a second blow. The body of the marionette quivered; her face remained unchanged.

Suddenly he pulled her out of the box, laid her on the bench, and holding her legs with one hand, began to rain blows on the nail, which seemed stubborn. Some of his blows went wide; there was a crash as the other arm broke and fell to the floor; but he did not stop. At last there was a rending crash which seemed to fill the shed, and the trunk split from top to bottom and lay in two halves on the bench. The head remained attached to one of these; the face was still unchanged.

"All right, then," said Hans, "we'll see."

He stood quite still; then he pointed the nail in the centre of the marionette's brow, raised the hammer, and, as if he had calculated the precise force of the blow, brought it down heavily on the nail. The marionette's head split in two in a straight line running from her hair, along one side of her nose, to her chin. One half of the head remained attached to the corresponding section of the trunk; this half was Gretchen now. Here brow, nose, eye, cheek, and chin were still serene and unfathomable. He let the hammer fall on the floor; he was no longer interested in what he had been doing. The chair faced away from the marionette; he sat down in it. For a little while he remained staring at the wall. He had not discovered anything; but he felt very tired. At last he rose. He saw the marionette chopped to pieces on the bench and realised what he had done. As he stood he could not take his eyes away from her face. The top of it was held together by her hair, but a cleft widened steadily from the brow and left at the chin a gaping space at which he gazed with fear. The marionette's eyes, which had fallen away from each other, looking in opposite directions, gave her face an idiotic, laughing expression. He ran out of the shed.

Sitting in his room, he realised that the other Hans and the other Gretchen had existed all the time. Now he had destroyed them, and he was terrified lest he should see the gutted house, with Gretchen and the other Hans lying dead in the garden. As he sat staring at the wall three rusty bars appeared between him and it; yellow-green flakes were falling slowly from them; he had looked for a few minutes before he realised that they were part of the railing which ran along the garden wall. Beyond them lay the garden, the house, and Gretchen and Hans; in another moment he would break in upon them; he looked around, afraid to let his eyes rest on any point. But presently he was gazing at the front of an old house; plaster was scaling from the walls; the windows were very dirty; he could see nothing through them. All at once his eyes rested on the steps before the door. It was the other house; in a moment the garden would lie before him; everything would be laid bare, and he would not be able to escape.

He went over to the bed and lay down with

his face to the wall, knowing that now he was about to see the garden and Hans and Gretchen, and that he could not escape. Presently he was looking at a heap of sodden brown leaves which seemed to be lying just in front of him, and he thought, This is the beginning. When he glanced up he saw that he was in the garden; heaps of leaves were lying everywhere on the grass, on the paths, and against the trunks of the trees. As he approached the nearest one it began to change (he had known it would change), and lying on the grass were two inanimate figures doubled up, their heads to their feet. Everywhere in the garden they lay, another Hans beside another Gretchen; and he saw now that in destroying the marionette he had destroyed a numberless host, who were harvested here. Presently an old man came out of the house; it was his father. He looked at the figures lying on the grass, went up to the first pair, straightened out their limbs, and began to carry them into the house. He did this for a long time, but the multitude lying on the ground remained unchanged.

Hans put his hands to his head; it felt hot, as if it were about to burst. Something was pressing down on his shoulders and choking him. It was his suit; he stared at it in fear and began to take it off.

Martin came into the room a little later. He found Hans walking about naked and beating his head against the wall. "All right! We'll see!" he was shouting.

CHAPTER XV

THE day after Hans's collapse Martin went down to the shed. He looked at the blocks of wood. "What shall I do with them?" he wondered. But he could think of nothing. Going back to the house, he took down the key, and returned to the shed and locked it.

Hans gradually recovered. He lay without speaking in his bed, and when Martin said anything knit his brow, as if only by a painful effort could he summon a reply.

One day while Martin was sitting in the room reading, he heard Hans saying to himself: " Fritz, Karl, and ——"; the last name seemed to elude him. As if he found pleasure in the words he repeated: " Fritz, Karl, and ——"

Martin looked up.

"Would you like them, Hans?" he asked.

Hans frowned and nodded.

Martin went down to the shed and returned with the dolls. Taking them to his bedroom, he washed their faces, brushed their hair and clothes, and returned to Hans.

"There!" he said, laying them down on the bed. Hans put out his hands for them, drew them near him on the pillow, and lay gazing at them. The sight of them seemed to trouble him; he sighed, putting out his hand and gently touching their faces and clothes. Soon he fell asleep, the dolls beside him on the pillow. After this he recovered more quickly.

In a fortnight more he was able to get out of bed. One warm afternoon Martin helped him downstairs and seated him in a chair which Emma had placed in the corner where the flowers grew. It was now the end of autumn; almost all the flowers had fallen; but a few stood glittering in the clear, still light. After his weeks in the sick-room the murmur of the town seemed loud to Hans here; the sky sprang up, spanned from horizon to horizon; away to the left, a small patch on the landscape, the little wooded hill of Hellbrünn was red and brown; it had been green when he saw it last.

As he grew stronger he began to go more to the garden, but he never ventured near the shed. Soon snow fell and kept him confined to his room. There he played with the dolls, disposing them seated in hollows which he kneaded in the quilt of the bed.

With the coming of spring he grew more animated, and remained for long times in the garden walking about. One day he asked Martin to take him up the Kapuziner Berg. Martin consented at once. When they reached the top, Hans looked down at Salzburg with his former delight, and laughed, turning to Martin. He's just the same as the first time I brought him here, thought Martin, and he wondered: Will it all have to begin again? He remembered all Hans's states since the first time they had stood there, and the complete illusoriness of his life sank into his mind. He resolved that he would not encourage Hans to understand or enjoy again. Far better if he were to remain completely insensible.

Hans still treated his dolls with a deliberate and wary gentleness. But when he was in the garden or on the hill his movements became restless; he seemed to be rebelling against his impotence. This disquieted Martin, and he closed himself into his study.

One night Hans had a strange dream. He dreamt that he was sitting in his room when the door opened and his father stood on the threshold. Martin was dressed in black; his hands were gloved, and in one of them he held his bowler hat. Without coming farther into the room he said in a carefully modulated voice, as if he were conveying a secret: " Come with me. Gretchen is dead."

When he heard this Hans was filled with wonder, and he rose and followed his father. Reaching the foot of the stairs, they turned into the dining-room. But here everything was changed, and he knew now that he was in a room in a house where he had never been before; it was the other house. The roof was very high; from where he stood in the doorway the polished floor stretched for an immense distance; in the light cast by two tall, curtainless windows spanned from floor to ceiling everything glittered. The room was empty save for a small bed islanded in the centre, around which, as if grouped for the effect, stood a few men in elegant black clothes, Faust and Mephistopheles among them. On the bed, dressed in white, her yellow hair falling over her breast, a girl was lying dead. When Hans appeared in the doorway, the mourners looked up and moved aside, and he thought: They are waiting for me! As soon as he knew this, something made him walk across to a marble mantelpiece near the door, lean his elbow upon it, and bow his head on his uplifted hand. Standing thus he began to weep, his back to the room. He wept on, the tears flowing from an inner source which had loosened, filling him with a desire to go on weeping until he should be free.

At last his tears ceased, he felt calm, and turning round he walked up to the bed through the watching mourners. Sitting down on a chair, he looked down at the dead girl. It was Gretchen, but she was very pale; the lines of brow, nose, and chin seemed so fragile that a breath might dissolve them; her eyes were closed; and she was almost as tall as he, as if in dying she had returned to her true form which through some great misfortune she had lost. As he looked her face seemed to flush imperceptibly. The glow was faint at first, tingeing her cheeks; but it deepened, and in a moment she burned in a fever, her cheeks flaming more violently as successive waves flooded them; until he was afraid lest she should dissolve in the intensity of the fire. The glow seemed to come from within her; but in reality it flowed from a centre, warm, limpid, yet of excessive radiance, in his own breast. This point in his breast, which was circular like a clear sun, seemed to heal all his body while it vivified the form lying on the bed. Presently Gretchen's eyes fluttered and opened; she held out her hand to him and smiled, her face radiant. Hans took her hand and arose.

"See! I have brought her to life!" he said in a solemn voice. But he stopped in terror.

"See! God has brought her to life!" he said, and fell on his knees beside the bed.

Suddenly he was no longer in the room. Gretchen's hand still in his, he was walking through a street of an old and deserted town. The sun was rising over the rim of the plain, and its rays streamed down the street, irradiating the walls of the houses, which stretched forward narrowing, on either hand, making a tunnel of light. Through this tunnel Hans seemed to be walking straight into the sun; he felt disembodied, as if the radiance were dissolving his lineaments into glittering beams. The cobble-stones at his feet shone, and looking down he saw tender green grass beginning to sprout between them. As he went on the grass grew with a regular, smooth sweep; the walls crumbled, sending out green branches from the stone; and in a little square where he was standing now, trees began to rise and blossom round him, filling the air with perfume, and he heard the plashing of water and the songs of birds. He wandered on among the green fields, Gretchen, still in her snowy grave-clothes, by his side. He awoke very much astonished.

While Martin was walking in the garden next morning he saw Hans go to the shed and try the door. The marionette is still there, he remembered, and going into the house he took down the key of the shed and put it in his pocket.

Later he tried to find out from Hans what he had wanted in the shed.

"I had a dream last night," replied Hans. He would not say anything more.

As Martin was turning away he asked, without looking at Hans: "Was the dream about Gretchen?"

Hans replied in his ordinary voice: "Yes."

"Well, what has happened to her?"

Hans looked at his father, and shook his head.

After Hans had gone up to his room, Martin went into the shed. He stood looking at the four pieces of wood; then he began to dust them, and carried them up to his study.

That afternoon he glued the marionette together. Except for the tiny holes in the centre of her brow and breast, she fitted together without a flaw. When the glue had dried, the holes were scarcely visible; the glue filled them in flush with the wood.

Martin now dressed the marionette, carried her down to the shed, and laid her in the box. Locking the door again after him, he went up to Hans's room

"I've found the key of the shed," he said. "Do you still want to go in?"

"Yes."

"Then come down with me now."

Hans followed his father. Martin inserted the key in the lock. Opening the door, he said: "Go inside."

Hans went forward and stood looking down at the marionette. Martin could not tell what was passing in his mind. Presently he ventured to say: "Well?"

Hans looked at him without speaking, then turned again to the marionette. He did not reply for a moment; but presently he glanced at his father and said: "I don't want her any more." His voice was calm. He looked at the marionette with an enquiring expression, as if he were surprised.

Martin did not try to interest him in the marionette again; he felt that this was the end of the episode. The yellow-and-green box continued to lie in the shed, and presently dust gathered on it.

Shortly after this the gardener whom Martin hired fell ill, and Martin had to take up his work. The first day while he was working in the garden, Hans came and stood watching him, and after a few minutes Martin asked if he would like to help. Hans learned quickly, and soon Martin left the work entirely to him.

When Emma saw Hans working in the garden, she would feel: "I have won." Martin seemed to accept his son now for what he was, without trying to change him. Yet sometimes he felt that his attempt had not been wasted and that without the aid of the marionettes Hans would not be so peaceful now.

Hans is at present between twenty and thirty. He is less afraid of people than he used to be, and may be seen, with his father, tramping the less frequented roads near Salzburg. Through long association father and son have come to resemble each other in their gestures and ways of speech. Emma is still with them.

AFTERWORD

When Edwin Muir, in the course of work on his autobiography, reread *The Marionette* (1927) for the first time in twenty years, it was not as he had expected it to be. He had written the novel, so he thought, out of love for the Salzburg where he and his wife had spent the autumn of 1923, yet now he found:

> that it did not tell me much about Salzburg but a great deal about the mingled excitement and fear which we feel on setting foot in a town which we have never seen before. The story is about a young half-witted boy called Hans, and Salzburg is seen through his eyes with the simplicity of one who does not understand what he sees. Obviously in presenting his fragmentary picture of the town I was resurrecting my own, for our first impressions of a new place are very like the first impressions of a child come new into the midst of new things.

In other words, vividly and specifically though it is evoked, Salzburg in Muir's novel stands for the world as we all have to discover it, as, in all its diversities and its intangible unity, it proffers itself to us. And in choosing for his central character Hans, a "half-witted boy", the author has consciously opted for the vantage-point of someone lacking in the information or the capacity for intellectual analysis; and who is therefore peculiarly open to the quiddity of places and objects and will interpret them solely according to his deepest psychic urges and needs. Hans's growing understanding (like an infant's, like the most innocent traveller's) comes through experiences that he has neither willed nor comprehended. Thus, during his first proper excursion into Salzburg, Hans feels menaced by the towering castle, the houses that seem about to topple down upon him, all the carts and horses and people. But when we take leave of him, we feel that, as a result of his increased familiarity with the place, some sort of pattern has emerged for him – and for us. Yet existential mystery still remains, just as it inevitably reasserts itself for a visitor when he leaves a place he has just got to know. This seems to me to be symbolised by Hans's wondering admiration of autumn's mark upon the wooded hill of the Hellbrünn at the book's close.

The above may suggest that *The Marionette* is primarily an expression of a poet's response to his travels, with Salzburg as a metaphor for life or adult experience, as, say, Venice is in L. P. Hartley's *Eustace and Hilda*. This is, however, only one aspect of the novel. It would be more accurate to see the investigation and metaphoric treatment of Salzburg as an immediately intelligible and accessible parallel for other investigations and metaphoric presentations. Far from being a mere journey to Salzburg, *The Marionette* – for all its wonderfully limpid style and seeming simplicity of presentation (mimetic of the hero's "simplicity") – is a demanding journey into man's psyche. However, before going further, it should be said that there were two particular features of the Salzburg Edwin Muir visited that played decisive parts in *The Marionette* as it evolved in Muir's mind.

First, Salzburg was, and is, the home of a unique and world-famous puppet theatre. This does not merely provide the controlling symbol of the novel, but is itself a focus for the author's universalising scrutiny. The second feature belongs to Muir's times: among so much that was lovely and life-enhancing (fittingly represented by Herr Hoffmann's theatre) Muir was deeply disturbed by one aspect of Salzburg life, its pervasive anti-semitism. A local paper, *Der Eiserne Besen* (*The Iron Broom*) propagated vile stories against the Jews, a bookseller grew angry when asked for Hofmannsthal's poems. With a poet's prescience Muir must have seen the full malignancy of this social cancer. It must surely have assisted him towards his choice of a "feeble-minded" hero, for the Nazis were to have no more room for the mentally defective in their Reich than for Jews, gipsies or gays. Hans becomes, thus, the very pattern of the congenitally non-conformist, by its attitudes to whom any society or creed must be judged. The vivid scene – one of the novel's turning-points – when Hans, engrossed in his own pursuits, is mobbed by cruel boys, with cries of "Loony! Loony!" and the hurling of stones, anticipates many terrible real scenes in between-the-wars Germany and Austria. Muir's prescience in Salzburg must indeed, I think, be responsible for the considerable attention given in *The Marionette* not only to the destructive, but to the sadistic impulses from the disturbed psyche.

The kind of inquiry *The Marionette* constitutes is, therefore, of a most ambitious kind, and it may be useful to understand something of Muir's ideas, preoccupations and situation when, two years after his stay in Salzburg, he began work on this extraordinary novel. Fortunately, we have the material for such understanding, for Muir wrote a wholly remarkable autobiography, first published as *The Story and the Fable* (1940) and then expanded into *An Autobiography* (1954). Childhood and boyhood in the Orkneys, in a tight-knit family, in as organic a community as any in Europe, close to nature, close to the generations of the dead, was followed, because of his father's economic difficulties, by a move to Glasgow. The shock of the sudden plunge into the life of a harsh, amorphous, poor industrial city was maybe the principal cause of the appalling tragedies of the next few years. He lost his father, the two brothers to whom he was closest, and his mother, and three of these four deaths occurred after great suffering. Muir, who had been "saved" at both Orkney and Glasgow revivalist meetings, and who had prayed hard for his nearest brother, Johnnie, now had to reject, or at least re-define, his concept of God. And meanwhile he had a living to earn, and took thankless, ill-paid jobs in the city; these lasted until he met his wife in 1919. During these years, for all his inner *angst*, he flung himself into socialist activities and into a self-education which resulted in a virtual "conversion" to Nietzscheanism. Muir became convinced that man must free himself through a syndicalist reorganisation of society in order to realise all that was within him: man, as we mostly encounter him, is a shadow of his real self. He is, to employ the imagery of *The Marionette*, a puppet instead of a free moving human being.

These elements of his Glasgow Nietzscheanism the Muir of

this, his first published novel, largely retained. One of its cardinal ideas, however, he did not; and yet, inverted, it does play a very important part in *The Marionette*. This is a principled rejection of pity as Christian orthodoxy understands it. Pity was felt to reduce and degrade its objects, and thus to be part of the arsenal of the propertied for preserving the status quo. In his autobiography, Muir interprets this youthful repudiation of pity as a necessary way of coping with his own pitiable state and with the tragedies of the loved members of his family. As he gradually moved towards a very inclusive Christianity, he valued more and more the compassion that came so easily to his gentle and kindly nature.

Muir's choice of an idiot as hero is deliberately *anti-*Nietzschean, as are the two decisive moments in Hans's hidden inner growth, when he feels deep and strong pity for Gretchen, the marionette. In the second, and redemptive, instance Hans realises what he has done to her and begins to weep, "the tears flowing from an inner source which had loosened, filling him with a desire to go on weeping until he should be free". Freedom comes directly from this discovery of compassion: Hans is, afterwards, able to live a harmonious life, his inner enemies vanquished. And yet, it seems to me, some of Nietzsche's "gay science" does survive in the book, for Hans the half-wit is rendered quite without the condescension of pity; for all his deficiencies he stands as dignified and as important as any other living being in the landscape revealed to us.

The early years of Muir's marriage – a very creative and loving one – brought about in him a terrible confrontation of both the events and the significance of his Glasgow life. This took him to the frontiers of breakdown and induced the kind of hallucinatory "waking dreams" attributed to Hans in the novel. Among other things, the confrontation led Muir to deny another Nietzschean doctrine, one which he had anyway always found difficult: that of Eternal Recurrence. In a later poem indeed – "The Recurrence" in *The Narrow Place* (1943) – he was feelingly to attack it:

> What has been can never return,
> What is not will surely be
> In the changed unchanging reign,
> Else the Actor on the Tree
> Would loll at ease, miming pain,
> And counterfeit mortality.

Muir clearly found it unbearable to think of himself and those dear to him eternally repeating all the pains of Glasgow, and, as readers of his poems will know, the image of life as a journey towards, and ending in, eternity took the firmest hold on his mind. *The Marionette* in its charting of the progress of both Hans and his troubled father towards a very real peace (a progress in which expeditions and long walks play key parts) can surely be viewed as a paradigm of the poet's development. Nevertheless, both here and elsewhere in Muir's work we can, I think, discover the legacy of Nietzschean Recurrence: in the preoccupation with what I would call Perpetual Reenactment. By this phrase I mean the idea that every one of us experiences in the inner life of imagination and dream, and in the outer one of occurrences, deeds and relationships, all the crucial events of man's history – those which are preserved for us in the ancient inheritance of myth. Two such mythic events call for particular attention here, the Fall and the Crucifixion ("the Actor on the Tree"). First, the Fall:

Muir's Orcadian childhood often acquired in his memory a prelapsarian light. And central to his mature thought is the concept of man's eventual recovery of Eden, but an Eden which will utilise all the energies and experiences of our fallen selves. (See the poem "One Foot in Eden".) Animals were always of the greatest importance to Muir. He believed that we still suffer guilt and undergo expiation for our severance from the original Adamic *participation mystique*. This we have to some extent conserved in fable, fairy-tale and heraldry. When in *The Marionette* we first meet Hans, he sees nature as a "terrifying heraldry": "The cat, the lizard, and the wasp were embattled forces armed for war, carrying terror and death on their blazoned stripes, their stings, claws and tongues." But by the novel's close he has, through events he cannot understand, won through to a harmony with nature: "trees began to rise and blossom round him, filling the air with perfume, and he heard the plashing of water and the songs of birds." This is a fitting prelude for his near-Adamic life as gardener. And the redemption I have alluded to has been effected surely by a most distinct version of the Crucifixion. Hans has punished with nails the innocent Gretchen, the beloved marionette, yet his savagery becomes his own crucifixion from which he will rise, merciful and purged, and at peace at last. All this has been heralded by one of the "waking dreams" which so clearly derive from Muir's own, a dream in which he saw "a small green hill", as in the Bible, glittering in the distance.

Muir's conviction that man's soul was eternal was the result of an inner process which began perhaps with a moment recorded in *An Autobiography*. Returning from work on a tramcar in the summer of 1919, Muir suddenly had a vision of every passenger as a spiritless beast: "I realised that in all Glasgow, in all Scotland, in all the world, there was nothing but millions of such creatures living an animal life and moving towards an animal death as towards a great slaughter-house." It is not hard to pass from this view of man to the image of the puppet and of other simulacra of human beings at the very centre of *The Marionette*. Muir was, of course, not alone among artists of the early twentieth century in his fascination with such artifacts and their symbolic and psycho-cultural significance. We have Stravinsky's Petrushka and Falla's *Retablo de Maese Pedro (Master Peter's Puppet-Show)*, Rilke's obsession with dolls (e.g. in the *Duino Elegies*) and de la Mare's poems about scarecrows. Allied to these are creations like Picasso's *Saltimbanques* and, again, the great attention this period paid to circus, masquerade, and mime. Hans, it will be recalled, puts on a marionette's suit like some vaudeville artiste. The puppet, clown and doll all immediately provoke speculations about reality versus illusion, the mask and the face, the persona and the real self, societised man and his primitive kin – debates so central to this phase of our history. They can also represent man without a soul, yet in comic/tragic need of one.

In *The Marionette* the themes above are subjected to

extraordinarily complex transformation and treatment. Hans becomes the possessor of three dolls, all male, of whom he is both master and servant. Martin, his father, at once to please and to educate him, gives him a dolls-house to accommodate them. It includes three miniature dolls, playthings for the dolls themselves. These, however, Hans despises, and he throws them away.

Next in his attempt to bring his half-witted son closer to what he conceives of as reality, Martin takes him to the marionette theatre, Salzburg's famous institution. The boy is as compelled by what he sees there – a performance of the famous Faust puppet-play which inspired Goethe – as he would have been as a spectator of such events in actuality. Indeed Hans does not perceive any difference. He takes the marionette characters of the Faust play into himself; they become as living companions to him, and alter his relation to the earlier dolls and, indeed, to all around him. In particular, one marionette (hence the singular form of the novel's title) preoccupies him; significantly this is a feminine puppet, Faust's Gretchen, the very embodiment of what men desire of women. At another performance of the Faust play in Herr Hoffmann's theatre, the Gretchen marionette has an accident. This horrifies and bewilders Hans and triggers off the cathartic sequence which culminates in the translated/reenacted crucifixion and resurrection that I have already mentioned.

Clearly it would be reductive to this closely worked and profound short novel to ascribe specific meanings to the human simulacra and to the permutations and progression of Hans's relation to them. However a few suggestions might not be inapposite. Cannot the three dolls, Fritz, Karl and the nameless one stand, respectively, for the ego, the id and the super-ego? And when we move to the world of the puppet-theatre, cannot we see Mephistopheles as the id, Faust as the super-ego and Gretchen, with her beauty and sanity, as the ego? She is also, of course, the anima, and Hans, we should remember, has moved in a set-up where woman has been represented only by the self-humbling servant, Emma.

The number three is of recurrent and dominating significance in the book: three dogs in that early experience of Hans's; three goldfish in a bowl; three dolls, as described above; only three characters of real concern, Hans, Martin and Emma. The novel moves, too, on three levels: Hans's relationship with, and education towards, the outside world; Hans's entanglement with the dolls and puppets; and Hans's own interior dreams and fantasies, often very charged and horrifying, and fed by both the exterior world and the puppet one. Both the second and the third of these levels have properties of both the super-ego and the id. What happens at these levels affects the first, the story of Hans's relation to Salzburg and to his father and Emma. The conclusion of this shows us the ego at peace, and, even though Hans is himself less than a normal human being as conventionally defined, it is not hard to see him, as we last receive news of him, as the owner of a soul, even (however we ourselves may reject the doctrine intellectually) of an *immortal* soul.

Thus, this short work, the result of a fairly brief visit to a city that played no great role in Muir's life, is, in truth, a very adventurous demonstration of how the psyche, in its interactions with the world outside itself, can achieve victory over chaos. *The Marionette* is an account, by one of the most truthful and noble-minded British poets of the century, of how – in Freudian terms – Eros, the impulse to love, can win over Thanatos, the movement towards death, without evading the latter's reality.

And in his drawing on our mythic inheritance, Muir shows us, in this tale of a half-wit and a puppet, how we must always see ourselves as part of a great and finally unknowable whole, made up of past as well as present, of (to use Muir's own terms) fable as well as story, how we must realise the destiny he was to set forth in his long poem "Variations on a Time Theme" of 1934:

> There is a stream
> We have been told of. Where it is
> We do not know. But it is not a dream,
> Though like a dream. We cannot miss

>   The road that leads us to it. Fate
>   Will take us there that keeps us here.
>   Neither hope nor fear
>   Can hasten or retard the date
>   Of our deliverance; when we shall leave this sand
>   And enter the unknown and feared and longed-for land.

Paul Binding, Anticoli Corrado 1986